THE DARK CRYSTAL
THE NOVELIZATION

Published by
ARCHAIA™

THE DARK CRYSTAL
THE NOVELIZATION

Based on the Jim Henson film

Adapted by
A. C. H. SMITH

Illustrations by
BRIAN FROUD
and the production design team at
Jim Henson's Creature Shop

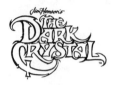

The Dark Crystal is based on the movie produced by Jim Henson and Gary Kurtz, directed by Jim Henson and Frank Oz, with David Lazer as executive producer, screenplay by David Odell, and conceptual design by Brian Froud.

Type Layout by **Scott Newman**
Cover Design by **Faceout Studio**
Additional Design by **Emi Yonemura Brown**
The Jim Henson Company Archivist, **Karen Falk**
Assistant Editor, Archaia Edition, **Cameron Chittock**
Editors, Archaia Edition, **Stephen Christy & Rebecca Taylor**

Special Thanks to Brian Henson, Lisa Henson, Jim Formanek, Nicole Goldman, Carla DellaVedova, Karen Falk, Blanca Lista, Shane Mang, and the entire Jim Henson Company team, Charles Brock, Torrey Sharp, Kelly Vlach, the entire Faceout Studio team, Sam Downie, Forrest Lighthart, and the Harry Ransom Center at The University of Texas at Austin.

CONTENTS

   I.   In the Forge of Thunder 11

   II.   On Aughra's High Hill 45

  III.   With So Many Questions 77

  IV.   In Country Mirth 95

   V.   At the Houses of the Old Ones 111

  VI.   To the Castle 129

 VII.   Into the Dark 145

VIII.   The Fire Below 163

  IX.   When Single Shines the Triple Sun 175

   X.   Behind A.C.H. Smith's The Dark Crystal Novelization...197

  XI.   Notes from Jim Henson on The Dark Crystal 201

THE DARK CRYSTAL
THE NOVELIZATION

Brian Froud

CHAPTER I
IN THE FORGE
OF THUNDER

There was only Jen. Jen alone.

His favorite game was to blow his flute and imagine other Gelfling, from just beyond the first trees, summoned by his music, creeping up behind him as he sat beside the waterfalls. They would be smiling because they would think they were hidden from Jen by the rocks. And when he stopped playing his flute and quickly turned around and caught sight of them moving, they would be obliged to stay with him then, and live with him forever, in the valley of the urRu.

It was only a game he played, on his own.

Below the waterfalls were the green pools in which he swam. He dived down to the weeds, then turned face-upward and floated very slowly back to the surface, watching the sunlight above him dance and shatter and dance again, like the hot metals in the pans urTih the Alchemist used. The creatures of the pools swam past him, unafraid, knowing him: the yellow and brown Myrrhie, the long, wriggling Krikids. Jen had always swum with them in their pools, ever since the urRu had brought him to their valley to live with them. He pretended that the creatures in the pool, and those on the land and of the air, were his friends. As they were, indeed, but friends with whom he could not converse. Only the urRu could speak Gelfling to him, and they always did, because their own language was too difficult for him to learn. The urRu were his real friends, of course, but it was difficult to think of them as friends: they were so immensely old and slow and huge and abstracted from everyday things.

Jen squinted at the sky. It was behaving strangely today.

They were kind to him, the urRu, even though they never cooked food he liked. He could not remember what Gelfling meals were, could only remember his mother as a shadow over his small body, but he was convinced that somewhere there was food he would relish. It did not grow in the valley, the urRu would answer if he questioned them. When he pointed to berries he would have liked to eat, they forbade him to, in fear he might be poisoned.

"Wise Ones," Jen would say—that was what their name meant, *urRu*, the old and wise ones–"won't your wisdom tell you if these purple berries are poisonous or not?"

They would shake their great mournful heads, thin grey hair brushing over their ears. "Wisdom is not for knowing but for understanding" was their answer. "Our food is good for you. It will suffice. We cannot know what is bad for a Gelfling. Eat up, and grow strong."

The urRu loved him, Jen knew that.

Outside the valley, with its rocks and cascading pools, its trees, berrybushes, flowers, and grasses, outside, beyond the boundary of the outer Standing Stones, there must be, he thought, a place where Gelfling food grew; a place where Gelfling had once lived, where he had lived when his mother and father were alive. He thought he could remember being among many Gelfling. Where had they all gone? He would ask, "Why may I not explore outside this valley?"

"You might lose your way," the urRu would reply.

"One of you could come with me."

"No, little one, we cannot leave the valley."

"Not ever?"

"Not yet."

"When, then?"

"Not yet."

"One day, will you? And may I come with you?"

"One day," they would say, "yes, one day you will leave here."

"When?"

At that they would raise their old, lined faces, look pensively at the sky, and walk slowly away.

Oh, how sad they seemed to Jen, those weary, kind faces of theirs.

"I would take my flute with me," he offered. "I would play it all the time I was outside the valley so that you could always come and find me again."

"Not yet, little one."

And so he stayed in the valley and played his flute. It was a double flute, and he had learned to play harmonies on it. The urRu encouraged him to practice, and he thought they must have given him the flute in the beginning. Anyway, he could not remember a time when he did not have it. Sometimes urSol the Chanter sang while Jen played. He was a fine musician, urSol, and could sing a third row of harmony, holding Jen cupped in his hand, by his head. The only difficulty they had was that urSol's voice was loud and deep, sufficient to make the rocks vibrate. To accompany quietly enough so that Jen's flute could be heard, he had to keep his mouth almost closed, in a sort of humming, and that, he said, was hard work.

The sky today disquieted Jen. The wind kept changing its direction, as he could easily tell from the different patterns of ripples fleeting across the surface of the pools. He had been woken up by thunder, although it was far away, and all day the sky had been rumbling. The Krikids were agitated in the pools. Once Jen had thought he felt the ground move, and had glimpsed something like a spark traveling across the valley and over the rim of rocks above it. It had gone so fast he could not be sure what it was. He had run along the spiral path, past the eighteen caves halfway up the cliff, to survey the valley. He thought he saw two or three more sparks flash across the land.

He wanted to ask his Master, urSu, what it all was. But urSu had not yet come out of the cave they shared, and Jen did not want to go in and disturb him if he was thinking.

The sky was turning black. Jen had seen storms before but none as dark as this. He remembered the day his mother had died. He was frightened of the darkness.

The ripples had altered again, and the thunder was getting louder. Only one sun was visible, and that was hazed by cloud. Jen decided that he would play on his flute. Harmony is the sound that goodness makes, urSol the Chanter said. Jen had to do something to answer the storm.

In a distant land, the storm raged across the sky above a brooding castle. Clouds boiled, purple, yellow, grey, black. Eerie lights glinted and vanished in momentary cloud caverns, lightning concussed the ground, and stray beams of sunlight swept across it like moving spokes. To the bleak crag on which the castle stood, now and then a pulse, a flash, surged across deserts, forests, ravines, craters, rivers, and mountains, along ley-lines of energy from the Standing Stones in the valley of urRu. It was as though the castle were sucking up the land's power to withstand the storm overhead.

Some borrowed or stolen force might have accounted for the persistence, in that furious sky, of one vent in the clouds directly above the central tower. Through the vent steadily shone one strong beam from the sun, at noon. The beam penetrated the castle tower through a triangular portal at its highest point.

Within the tower it directly struck a huge crystal, wine dark in color, suspended in midair by its own gravity. The Crystal was quartz-like, with threefold symmetry, rhombohedral at its top and base. But what had once had a mineral magnificence was now cracked, decaying. Near the top was a cavity where a sliver of the Crystal, a shard, was missing altogether.

From the Crystal, the light was refracted into separate beams, which slanted sharply downward. The beams nearest to vertical traveled on down a shaft cut in the living rock, at the foot of which, deep beneath the Crystal, they met a lake of fire. Around the shaft opened a vast ceremonial chamber, triangular in shape, and there the Crystal's refracted beams created a circle of pools of dark radiance on the floor.

Nine of the pools of light were vacant. In each of the other nine beams stood the sinister, reptilian figure of a Skeksis. All of them, with hooded eyes uneasy above their beak-like jaws, were surreptitiously watching the door. In the thick layers of robes with which they had draped their skinny, scaly bodies over eons, never removing a layer but adding another as one decayed, they stood bulky and almost motionless, imbibing the cosmic radiance from the Dark Crystal above them with a kind of thirst; but their unblinking eyes were not still, and their talons twitched as they watched for their Emperor.

Had he the strength to join them in the ceremony? If so, the sun's rays, enriched and vibrant from the Crystal, might revive him for the brief period until the Great Conjunction; and the power he would take on then would sustain him for eons more. If he was unable to join them now, he would not live long. In that event, one of the nine would become the new Emperor.

The design of the floor where the Skeksis stood was a spiral maze. An eye tracing it would eventually return to the point of the pattern from which it had started, except that the maze, being spiral, would appear to flow into a third dimension. It had no end and therefore no beginning, yet it progressed. Thus it was timeless, infinitely present, and so could be taken to be a representation of time, which cannot be pictured by those who imagine themselves linear subjects to it. The pattern of the spiral maze, subtly varied, connected the floors of all the ceremonial chambers in the castle.

The triangular walls of the Crystal Chamber, rising to meet at the open portal high above the crystal, had been fashioned by fine masons, honest to their craft. Throughout the reign of the Skeksis in that place, ugly embossments had been added, grotesque carvings made in the stone, symbols defaced, gaudy cloths and painted insignia hung, all emblems of power: the pentacle, the nine-pointed star, the four phases of the secret moon of Thra, the tetraktys, hexagrams, pyramids, tetrahedrons, double helices, left-handed and right-handed spiral swastikas, the alchemical symbols of the four elements and the three principles of nature, and, most obsessively pictured, a triangle containing three concentric circles, the icon of the Great Conjunction. Throughout the castle, along its dark passages, through arches and aisles, in chambers large and small, in the filthy dungeons and cells drenched in death, that triangular icon was to be seen, a pilgrim's talisman, a hunter's supplication, a prisoner's reckoning.

In the ceremonial chamber, the pools of light lost their radiance.

The sun had passed over. The Skeksis began to stir their swaddled bodies again, walking on their hind legs, forelegs poised in the air, talons arched, their heads, protruding from the humped cowls, thrust out as if to strike. They watched each other closely.

The Emperor had not appeared.

SkekNa the Slave-Master nodded a signal to a balcony built into the rock high up beside the Crystal. A cover was slowly closed across the triangular portal at the summit of the tower.

Outside the castle, the storm started to intensify. A creature that might have been a bird or a bat rose into the air from the battlements. In its claws it clutched a small piece of crystal, as it flew away across the landscape, its wings beating with slow deliberation. Another creature of the same breed followed it, and others still heading off in different directions, each grasping a piece of crystal.

The storm was closer to the valley now. Jen looked up at the sky. Its colors were reflected on the shivering pool. Soon he would have to find shelter in one of the vacant caves along the spiral pathway. For the time being, he willed himself to stay beside the pool, above the waterfall, playing the flute, until the last possible moment. His quiet, secure life among the urRu seldom presented him with the opportunity to be a little brave.

He leaned forward and gazed directly down into the pool. "Is that a brave face?" he asked himself aloud.

Although the water was not still, he knew his face well enough to see it plainly reflected on the shifting surface. Under the fringe of thick, dark hair was a countenance made almost triangular by the wide cheekbones tapering to a small chin. His large eyes were set well apart, on either side of a flattish nose. His Gelfling face was framed by long

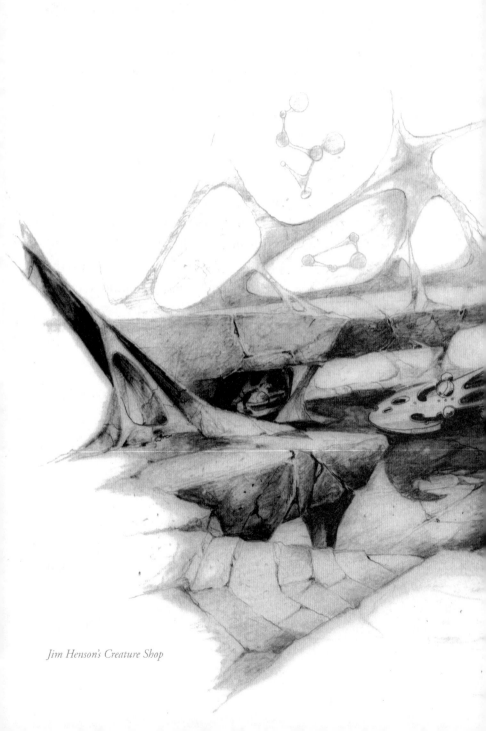

Jim Henson's Creature Shop

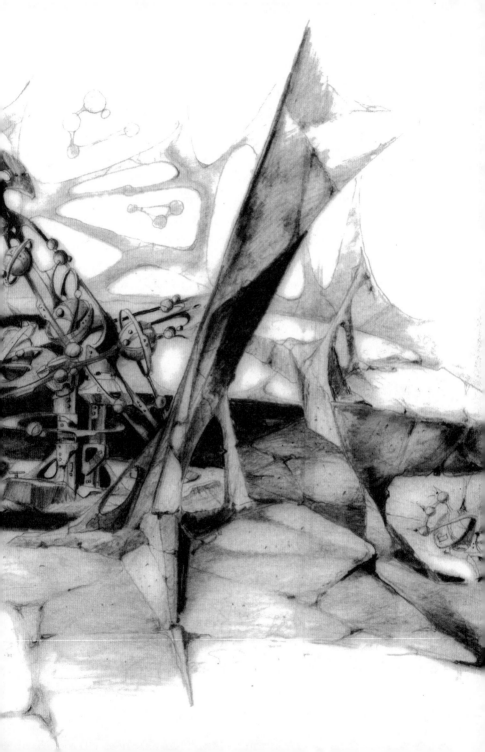

hair, through which his pointed ears protruded.

"A brave face?" He had asked that question often enough, and others. A handsome face, was it? An intelligent one? Sad? Stern? Was it even memorable?

All he had for comparison were the lugubrious faces of the urRu. Their aged, wrinkled eyes were so different from his bright ones. The skin on their faces was old, deeply lined in runic patterns. Their faces were not even in the same place as was Jen's but thrust forward on long, thick necks that were covered with manes of gray hair. When they walked, with their heavy, slightly swaying gait, on their two powerful legs, their massive long tails were not heavy enough to counterbalance the weight of their heads. They had to lean on walking sticks, which they held in front of them with one of their pairs of forearms, while their hind arms hung down toward the ground. Their heads were ponderous with wisdom, perhaps, or with memory, or with listening.

Their immensely slow and considered movements were made weightier yet by the garment each of them wore, something between a coat and a saddle blanket. These garments had been made for them by urUtt the Weaver and were fashioned to the individual by the system of knotting threads he used. The complex pattern of knots formed a cybernetic store for each wearer's thoughts, be they the medicinal knowledge of urNol the Herbalist, the astronomic records of urYod the Numerologist, the macrobiotic balances of urAmaj the Cook, or any other of the bodies of erudition that the urRu had been collecting for many eons. The garments were dusty and worn with age, but the colors had remained fast and the threads had not frayed because urUtt had used no scissors.

How could Jen ever have learned about himself by comparison with creatures so entirely different and so much larger—a hundred times heavier, quite probably? Everything they had taught him, which was a great deal, had been taught by precept. They could give no examples, not only because of their different physical beings, but also because the knowledge they had was absolutely conceptual. Nothing happened, nothing was apprehended, but it was instantly translated by the urRu into an idea and matched with all the other ideas accreted over the eons like all the dust on their garments. The spirals and runes in the skin of their heads were the grooves of coded thought, representing a symbolic interpretation of each urRu's total past, from which, at any moment, the future might have been projected by one who could systematically construe the signs. The habitual sadness of their expressions and the marked slowness of their low, resonant speech were evidence of their cerebral natures. Anyone who had never met the urRu might have supposed, at first, that they labored under a collective guilt, such was their lack of spontaneous action.

"A brave face?" Jen shrugged and sat down again. The storm was heading inexorably in the direction of the valley. The sky was darker now, and a chill edge in the air heralded the first rainfall.

Jen played a tune, trying to finger harmonies that might answer the thunderclouds. He double-stopped one pipe of the flute, as a kind of chanter, and on the other experimented with the quarter-tone effects he had discovered by partial stopping. He tapped his foot in a slow rhythm, shut his eyes, and improvised a sinuous melody. *Da da da datta da datta da da.*

When lightning cracked nearby, Jen opened his eyes again. Someone was behind him and towering over him, someone he had not heard approaching. He turned around quickly.

It was urZah the Ritual-Guardian, standing up straight on his haunched legs, his four arms spread-eagled, with his cane pointing to the sky.

"Pardon, Ancient One," Jen said, fearing his flute had interrupted urZah's thinking. "I did not mean to disturb you." Although, Jen reasoned, surely even an urRu's contemplation might be penetrated by a storm such as this.

UrZah answered in the fashion of the urRu, very slowly, with long pauses. "To mean is not to do," he said. "To make a sound"–he reflected for a long time–"is to trouble the roots of silence. To play the flute is… to make a slave of the air."

Jen turned away impatiently. "I know," he replied. "You've told me that before."

At once he wished he had not sounded the note of rudeness. It was not that he had any fear of punishment. In all his time with the urRu, none of them had ever chastised him, however subtly. Whenever he had spoken or behaved badly, the worst that had ensued, after a long meditative pause, was a somber sentence of philosophical correction. He doubted, in fact, that it was possible to upset one of them. No, he regretted what he had said only because it muffled the genuine respect he felt for urZah and all the others. Still, as the urRu themselves quite often said, a word spoken is a step taken.

Jen sat there, feeling awkward. He fingered his flute but thought he had better not play in case it was offending urZah. The urRu had not made a move but was still standing over Jen, his head cocked. Then he said, "In your cave there is one who has need."

"My Master?" Jen asked. He stood up, with a little stab of anxiety. His Master, urSu, had never before sent for him in the middle of the day. Why now?

UrZah was gazing at the sky. "The storm comes," he observed. "It is time. Time of change." He paused. "Time of trial."

So that was it. Something was to change and be tested. That was what the storm portended. Jen looked into urZah's weary, kind face and nodded hesitantly. He had always known that this day, sooner or later, would come. The skills and intuitions that the urRu had cultivated in him, while sheltering his childhood, were always designed to prepare Jen for some task. The urRu had never told him what the task would be; and, truth to tell, Jen had never pressed them for an explanation. With all his wishing that things could be altered, that the urRu would let him roam more freely, and especially that all the other Gelfling would come back and live with him, he did not want to lose what he had.

He ran up the spiral pathway. He was only just in time. The storm was breaking on the valley now. The wind! It was blowing about more than dust and spray from the waterfalls. The very stones were being shaken by it. Jen could feel little pebbles pattering on his skin.

Why were urIm the Healer, urNol the Herbalist, and urSol the Chanter standing together outside the cave Jen shared with urSu? Was there danger in this storm? What were they talking about?

The three urRu moved aside, slowly, to let him pass. What must it be like for them, he wondered, to be so heavy and slow, and see one running as fleetly as he did?

Now his Master would tell him why the sky was turbulent. Such black force, scudding clouds that seemed to have a purpose. It was a day like none he had ever known, and he did not like it. Whatever it was that the storm wanted of him, nothing in his life would ever again be as it had always been.

"Master, here I am."

As Jen stepped into the cave, through the entrances carved with the most elaborate runes of all the caves along the pathway, the storm outside rose to a crescendo of gale and rain and thunderclaps.

Jen paused for a moment beside his own small bed, carved into the wall of the cave, while his eyes and ears and breathing attuned themselves. He could see his Master at the rear of the cave, draped across the sleepframe that supported his massive weight. That was another strange occurrence today. His Master never rested during the daytime but was always at work with his books and his instruments, or conferring with other urRu.

"Master?"

UrSu, his head in an awkward position, stirred and looked up at Jen.

"Master, what does this storm mean?"

UrSu gestured weakly for Jen to draw nearer.

When he had done so, Jen experienced an alarm much greater than that which the storm had caused him. UrSu was prostrate. His breathing was labored and noisy. His eyes seemed cloudy and unable to focus clearly on Jen. His face was pale.

"Master, what is wrong?"

UrSu panted for breath before he could answer. "I was born…" he said, and the rest of the sentence was a mumble.

Jen cocked his head to indicate that he had not understood. His Master waved his hand to ask for patience. He struggled to bring his breathing under control.

"I was born under a shattered sky," he finally got out.

Jen swallowed hard, forcing himself to remain calm. "Please," he said, "it's me, Jen."

Again the Ancient One waved his hand with impatience. His mouth moved, shepherding the words. "A Crystal sang…" He breathed heavily in. "A Crystal sang to the three made one. The dark column, the rose column, and… and the radiance… itself."

Jen moved closer, leaning down to speak.

His Master muttered, "Listen. You must understand. You *must…*

After nine hundred and ninety-nine trine plus one trine... The Great Conjunction, the Crystal sang... I was born, ah, Skeksis, too..."

Jen stood there quite wretched, afraid of the changes in his life, and bewildered by the responsibility that he felt his Master's laborious muttering was imposing on him. He had no idea what he was to do with these fragments of knowledge—if knowledge they were and not merely the pointless ravings of someone mortally sick—any more than he could imagine what he ought to do to help his Master now.

"You are ill," Jen said. "You must rest."

If he could calm his Master, he would go fetch urIm the Healer, who, with his sense of an aura, could lay on hands, and perhaps everything would be right again.

UrSu took no notice. "Thrice times six were the urSkeks," he went on, with a kind of chanting rhythm to conserve his breath. "Dark the Crystal, oh... Shattered the sky, great pain, the Skeksis, they... Evil, dark, their rule..."

Jen was trying to concentrate on the torn words, in obedience to his Master's injunction to understand, but at the same time he was miserable with the realization that urIm, whom he had seen outside the cave, must already have visited the Master and left because there was nothing more he could do there.

"Great power," urSu continued, with a new access of breath, "not again, not renewed, not Skeksis, not if Gelfling, you, ah..." He groaned with the pain of his sickness. "You, make it whole, you must, you must, all whole, Gelfling. Again."

Drawing on his last reserves of strength, urSu raised his arm and held it over a copper bowl of liquid that was on the floor beside his sleepframe. His three long fingers and thumb pointed at the surface of the liquid, which at once turned cloudy. Outside the cave, a bolt of lightning struck with such force that Jen felt the ground shudder beneath him. Then, bemused, he watched the bowl of liquid, for it was forming itself into a shape, an image, a picture of a mountain. On top of the mountain he could plainly see a curiously domed building.

UrSu's eyes were shut fast. All his remaining energy was now concentrated into forming the picture in the bowl and the words he still struggled to speak. "A wanderer may come," he muttered. His voice was faint, but by now Jen's ears had attuned themselves. "Come from under the mountain bringing murder and birth."

"Master…" In Jen's voice was bewilderment and tenderness. He was close to tears.

UrSu clenched his fingers and released them with an alacrity that was out of keeping with the rest of his inert body. The clouded picture in the bowl changed. What took its place was the image of a piece of crystal, a dagger-shaped fragment, which glinted in the cloudy liquid below the urRu's pointing fingers.

"Mark this crystal shard," urSu intoned in a faint, distant chant. "An orphan must restore it. Heal the wound at the core of being. Wanderer, orphan, Gelfling, Jen, with this tool you may forge a fate. Now"–urSu's eyes flickered open to look at Jen–"now you are alone."

The image of the dagger-shaped crystal shard faded beneath urSu's fingers. At the moment of its disappearance it sounded a high-pitched ring of two notes, which sang around the walls of the cave, then died away very slowly. All that was left was the noise of urSu's heavy breathing. The liquid in the copper bowl had evaporated. UrSu's hand hung down limp.

"Alone?" Jen asked. "But what about you? What about all the urRu? Master…"

The ancient urRu's eyes were shut fast again. In a voice that sounded as though it came from the threshold of another world, he said, "Your journey must begin. The three brother suns will not wait." He paused. "Remember me, Jen. We may meet again, but not in this life."

Jen said nothing. He knew that words would be wasted. He stood, his face very still, aware of his small breathing in comparison with the gasping sound that came from his Master.

The storm continued to rage around the castle of the Dark Crystal. Through the dark halls of the castle swaggered the most massive and brutal of the Skeksis: skekUng the Garthim-Master, decked in a robe of armor pieces that glittered and rattled as he marched. His spurs struck sparks from the stone floor. The mad, cold eyes and the yellow fangs, revealed in a characteristic sneer, aroused a prehistoric fear in all who saw him, even in the other Skeksis. He was unusual among them in having held his position ever since their reign had begun. As their numbers had dwindled, from eighteen to ten, Skeksis had been promoted to fill the offices that had fallen vacant. But this was always and ever the Garthim-Master, from the first the strongest and most violent of them. The Garthim, he maintained, were his creation. To him was due all the honor for the foul instrument by means of which the Skeksis had tyrannized the land. They were the strike force of the Skeksis, huge and black-carapaced, mighty-clawed, like giant fleas with their dangling tentacles. Always some were standing like sentries along the corridors of the castle, lifeless until activated by a command. Others were held in reserve in a pit beneath the castle floors. The Garthim were scarcely creatures at all, more like the impulses of a cruel brain made over into crustacean objects, nightmare crabs, swift monsters designed for one purpose only: destruction. For any one of them there was no singular noun. They were the plural extensions of one will of evil. The

Garthim-Master took fierce pride in them.

Now he was marching to claim the reward he had been awaiting all these centuries: the throne. Everyone could see the Emperor was dying. This time, no other Skeksis would be able to resist the Garthim-Master's accession.

As he approached the ornate doorway of the Emperor's bedchamber, he was startled by the sudden appearance of skekSil the Chamberlain, who insinuated himself into the middle of the corridor in front of him. In spite of himself, the Garthim-Master hissed, in a moment of alarm, and hesitated. Then he snorted and strode resolutely on, past the only Skeksis who might oppose him as the new Emperor.

The Chamberlain stayed where he was, twisting his scrawny neck around to watch the Garthim-Master. He turned then and followed him toward the doorway, his moist and unctuous body more obsequiously bowed as he entered the imperial bedchamber. Under his arm he carried scrolls and administrative papers. He knew the dying Emperor would be in no condition to attend to them, but he wished to remind the other Skeksis of his official position: the Chief Secretary, and therefore next in line to the throne.

He eyed the rest of the Skeksis, assembled around the sumptuous bed, and smiled at each one of them with oily suspicion. The Garthim-Master's ambition was plain, but would any of the others make a bid?

Not the Slave-Master, with his patch to cover a mucid eye-socket and his hook for one hand. He had no fitting experience for it, no imagination, no nobility at all. Certainly not skekAyuk the Gourmand, who was too slovenly and slothful to care. Nor skekEkt the Ornamentalist, whose decadence and perversion could never command obedience. And least of all skekOk the Scroll-Keeper, that vacant idiot who continually mumbled to himself.

That left three to consider, and scuttle. SkekShod the Treasurer was no dangerous threat, being administratively subordinate to the Chamberlain and knowing nothing of executive responsibility. All he knew was how to bite gold. SkekTek the Scientist, however, was another matter. The others feared him because they could understand nothing of his work. He had amputated his own leg and arm in order to fit himself with appliances he had invented that were more powerful than the natural limbs. Likewise, he had cut out part of his circulatory system and substituted a series of exposed, transparent tubes in order to study the operation of his own blood and juices. Some thought him demented, and he was distrusted by all. Surely he would not be in contention.

Finally there was skekZok the Ritual-Master. Yes, the Chamberlain aimed a special smile at him. With his hieratic dignity and his unmatched knowledge of the symbols, the cards, the auguries, and the rituals, there was no denying that the Ritual-Master could be a formidable contender. And yet, he had never given any indication of coveting the throne. Until now, at least, he had always seemed satisfied with the spiritual, cabalistic power he unquestionably exercised. He might well have no taste for the fight, which would surely be a vicious one, were the Garthim-Master to persist in his vain, absurd pretensions.

The Emperor lay on his bed, his face dark against the white pillow and growing darker all the time, like a withering plum. The Skeksis knew what that portended. The imperial eyes were dull, unfocused. His breath rasped in his long throat, and his mouth gaped for air. Across the counterpane his hands were rambling, fingers twitching, as though they were seeking something firm to grasp. In one hand was the jeweled scepter, loosely held. Nine pairs of eyes watched it. None of the Skeksis said a word, but all of them were raptly attentive to every sound and motion. The Chamberlain edged closer, in readiness.

Brian Froud

When the scepter rolled out of the Emperor's feeble hand and lay on the counterpane near the edge of the bed, the Chamberlain moved in. He stretched out his hand for it, extending the long talons. The Garthim-Master jerked, taken by surprise. He stiffened, prepared to engage in an unseemly tussle with the Chamberlain.

But the Emperor's eyes were suddenly wide-open and ablaze. His neck whipped from the pillow; and his jaws, full of yellow teeth, snapped like a trap an inch away from the Chamberlain's outstretched hand.

The Chamberlain withdrew his talon with as much dignity as he could muster. "Your Imperial Majesty," he said in the wheedling voice that all the others loathed, "I merely wished to restore the symbol of supreme office to your hand, where it rightfully belongs. It would be shameful were we to allow the scepter of state to fall on the ground."

The Garthim-Master laughed under his breath, loudly enough to be heard at the end of the corridor. The Emperor's spiteful lunge proved to be the last action of a life passionately devoted to malevolence. He collapsed back onto the pillow and fell into a coma. The only evidence of enduring life was a small rattling noise in his chest. Then that stopped.

A black membrane slid over his eyes. Outside the castle, the last of the thunder died away.

Looking furtively around, the Chamberlain caught the eyes of both the Garthim-Master and the Ritual-Master, each of them similarly furtive. Well, now he knew, then. Three of them. If only the vicious old brute had confirmed the Chamberlain's natural succession there would have been no trouble. The Garthim-Master, like all who are competent at giving orders, was also punctilious in obeying them. As for the Ritual-Master, he would not have dared to question the expiring Emperor's command, else all his authority would have slipped from him, founded as it was on the mysteries of hierarchy, precedence, and predetermination. There would be a contest now.

Apart from the aspirants, the other six Skeksis had kept their gaze fixed upon their defunct Emperor. His corpse was decomposing with remarkable haste, having no soul to arrest the process. It was like the creation of volcanic rock within the space of a minute or two. His flesh seemed to boil, rise, blacken, and then transform into rock that rapidly developed gaping cracks and festering caves. Soon it crumbled into pebbles. A sour, grey dust thinly filmed the air.

Night came in fast, faster than an eye could adapt itself to starlight, and, later, to the small, pale-mauve moon. For a while the land was immersed in a darkness like ink. It was the time when every creature would fall quiet.

From deep within the labyrinthine bowels of the castle, strains of solemn music arose. It was a dirge in three-part harmony, sung by a chorus of slaves situated in choir stalls at the side of the mausoleum. All the Skeksis' slaves were captured Pod People, small and simple folk. Their voices had been alto in their natural state. Some of them, however, had been converted into lower registers by the Scientist, who for hundreds of years, had experimented with the excision and implantation of vocal cords, and now felt he had achieved just the right blending of parts.

He had no ear for music himself, but the Slave-Master did claim to have one and had taken responsibility for selecting and providing promising Pod specimens to the Scientist. The result of the experiments were delivered over to the Ornamentalist, who was in charge of rehearsals. He made a further selection, incorporating those he liked into the chorus and destroying the rest. The final arbiter was the Ritual-Master, since the chorus sang only on ritual occasions. A harsh judge, he had been known to cross the chamber and tear the head off a singer who failed to sing his part in tune. That it had happened less often of late was the reason why the Scientist felt that, in this field of experiment, he had been successful.

It had been the Scroll-Keeper's job to collect the Emperor's remains and coagulated fluids from among the vacated robes lying on the deathbed, where the scepter lay beside them. The remains were wound in cerements and sealed inside an ebony casket, tetrahedral in shape, bearing on all four sides silver icons of the triangle containing three concentric circles. The casket was then borne into the mausoleum by the Ritual-Master, the Chamberlain, and the Garthim-Master, one at each corner. The other six Skeksis followed in a single file: the strutting Slave-Master, the limping Scientist, the Treasurer wringing his hands, the Ornamentalist dressed in peacock silks and rich jeweled pieces, the Gourmand, wiping the corners of his mouth, and last the Scroll-Keeper, who had arrived late.

In arranging the procession, the Ritual-Master, the Chamberlain, and the Garthim-Master had disagreed over which of them should precede the others by bearing the foremost corner of the casket. The Ritual-Master argued that he was officiating at the ceremony; the Chamberlain pointed out that, at least for the present, he was the senior functionary of the state; and the Garthim-Master insisted that he had the chief-executive responsibility for maintaining order and security. In view of the sepulchral occasion, they found a temporary compromise, although each of them knew that it would not long outlast the Emperor's funerary casket.

As they trod the spiral maze of the mausoleum floor, the three of them also wheeled gravely around the axis of the casket in their hands, in a stately measure. The Pod People slaves, singing in the choir stalls, would have laughed at the spectacle had they been capable of laughter.

The procession threaded its spiral way to the center of the mausoleum, which was lit by urns whose flickerings cast grotesque shadows across the great vaulted room.

The Ritual-Master, the Chamberlain, and the Garthim-Master laid the casket on a broad obsidian catafalque, draped in black silk shot through with threads of gold. The Ritual-Master assumed his position at the head of the catafalque. The Chamberlain and the Garthim-Master withdrew to join the other Skeksis in a circle around the catafalque.

The Ritual-Master raised his eyes and intoned, "*Kekkon, Kekkon, Yazakaide, Akura, Kasdaw.*"

The rest repeated it after him.

Then the Ritual-Master shook his bony claws free of his robes and pointed at the Treasurer, who stood immediately to his right in the circle.

"*Hokkvatta skaun Kherron,*" the Treasurer responded, leaning forward and bowing his head.

The rest repeated it in unison.

And so, around the circle, while the chorus of slaves chanted quietly, each Skeksis intoned the same phrase, which all then repeated, in a rite consigning their Emperor's soul, which had never existed, to the protection of a higher being, in which none of the Skeksis could have tolerated belief. It was a ceremony of reassurance to the survivors. It was also an opportunity for the Chamberlain and the Garthim-Master to vie with each other in expressing their piety of homage. Both were resentful of the advantage the Ritual-Master had in the matter.

At a signal from the Ritual-Master a slave came forward, bearing around the circle a large copper bowl ornamented with silver. From it, each Skeksis took a smoking orb made of a translucent material that glowed with some inner combustion.

They faced the casket. "*Kekkon, Kekkon, Yazakaide, Akura, Teedkhug!*" the Ritual-Master screeched, raising his talons high above his head.

The choir's voices swelled to a climax. The Ritual-Master let his hands fall to his chest, and simultaneously the rest of the Skeksis threw the glowing orbs into the catafalque, crying "*Haakhaon!*" in their harsh, croaking voices. The catafalque was at once transformed into a pyre, blazing with the white brilliance of a dying star.

The Skeksis stood in a silent, watching circle as the gold-shot silks were consumed in flames and the casket was reduced to smoldering embers.

In the cave Jen stood quite still for a long time, gazing at the empty, runic garment on the sleepframe. He had seen death before, among the small creatures of the valley, but it had never been like this. His Master had seemed to evaporate, like a pure spirit. It was as though that weighty body had never been more than an idea in the mind of whatever it was that inhabited the flesh, an idea that had now been forgotten, discarded. Whatever it was had passed on to another, invisible idea. Would that be in here? Jen wondered. Or somewhere else? He knew that for a long time, perhaps forever, he would have the sense that his Master was present wherever he went, always walking beside him. He could not have brought himself to say anything that urSu would not have liked to hear.

The grief went deep in Jen, but deeper still, beneath it, he detected something hard. It was difficult to define, but it felt like courage: a new power in him, a new confidence. He examined it gingerly. He was afraid to learn exactly what it was in case it turned out to be pride, the guilty, arrogant joy of those who have survived. But he thought courage would be something more gentle than that. He would wait and get to know it. How strange, he reflected, that at a time of calamity he should gain something simple and strong and, perhaps, precious. Were all good and true lessons to be learned only at such cost?

How long he stood there he did not know, but eventually he turned and walked to stand in the mouth of the cave, looking out over the valley. The storm had cleared away, leaving behind it a sky scrubbed clean and blue. The creatures of the valley were running around, sniffing the sunshine. Down below, in the thalweg, the bottom of the valley, he could see the urRu, gathering around the Standing Stones that formed a triangle there.

Directed by urZah, they set out what was necessary for a funeral. Down the spiral path, from urSu's cave, they had carried his coat, which the process of dematerialization had now reduced to a cobwebby thing, frail and dry, an abandoned chrysalis. This, together with his few other personal belongings, they placed at the foot of the tallest of the stones. On another stone, which lay flat in the center of the triangle, they laid his walking stick, the Master's staff of office, totemically carved from one thick branch of hard nutwood. At the upper end of it was inset a small, perfectly formed rock crystal.

For hours they calculated the precise positions of the remaining objects that were needed to furnish the funeral ceremony: small fetishes, prayer sticks, stones, feathers, and pots. Watching them make the arrangements, Jen finally became impatient, in spite of his grief over the occasion. Throughout his life among the urRu, at the edge of his gratitude for their kindness to an orphan he had felt himself quietly chafing at their immensely patient attention to detail. What they called their "work" seemed to him to connect one thing to another. Sometimes it was quite literal. He had seen urNol, with his eye-patch and splintered finger, spend days on end with a pebble and four blue feathers, seeking to discover all the permutations that could result from binding the objects together with a length of string.

Other connections the urRu made were figurative. When the wind was in a certain quarter, it blew down the spiral path; and filling tunnels and passing the mouths of caves, it resounded through the valley like a reed pipe. At such times, the urRu never tired of arranging their own bodies to stop some of the cave mouths so that the pitch of the wind would be modulated. Why bother? Jen wondered. On his own little bifurcated flute he could demonstrate the same effect and play a melody at the same time.

In their collective obsession with rituals there was something slavish about the urRu. It affected everything in their lives, even the ordinary business of a day—sleeping, eating, walking, talking. It was always too slow for Jen, this labored, mannered, painstaking connection of things. What was the point? Turned inward, away from the world, they were, Jen thought, collectors of knowledge for its own sake. Why did they never *do* anything with it? Why could they not make the only connection that seemed to him useful: applying all their knowledge to change the world?

As he had grown older, he had tried, politely, to press his Master for the answers. UrSu, however, had simply traded concepts. One's body was a rehearsal of the history of the world. What one ate and thought was one's future. "The better you know me," urSu had said, "the better you will know the world as it will be without me."

And now Jen faced a world without urSu.

The new spark of confidence he had, to his surprise, found in himself at his Master's death was still there within him. But confidence to what end? "To forge a fate," urSu had said as he lay dying. "To heal the wound. To make it whole." What fate? What wound? What was expected of him? He had never been able to envision a future for himself except one in which his infant memories—his mother, father, other Gelfling—would become realities again. But whenever he had wished for that to happen—lying in bed at night, closing his eyes, pressing together the tips of his thumbs and forefingers—his concentration on those memories had led straight through to something he feared— some blackness, cruel pain, weeping. Was the past always stalking the present, waiting to destroy it? UrSu had told him that a two-dimensional question like that had no solution, and therefore no meaning. "Make a triangle with a past, present, and future. Then each two will explain the third."

"Nothing is except energy," urSu had said another time. "Energy exists only when a connection can be made. Connect one to one, and you will have energy that will serve your life. Connect one to one to one and nothing will ever be the same again. Look at my face, Jen. What you see was born when three were made one. Look harder now, harder than you have ever known how to look, and you might see that three will be made one again."

"What do you mean, Master? It is hard to understand. Can you not put it more simply?"

"It is already as simple as it can be. That is why you find it hard to understand."

Toward the end of the night, the urRu awaited the dawn, the twilight in which a spirit feels most at peace. Their funeral ceremony was prepared. Seven of them sat in positions that, together with the three Standing Stones, formed a tetraktys. Set apart on one side was urUtt, with a harp; facing the rest from a knoll behind the tallest stone at the apex of the triangle was urZah. Jen, sitting beside him, was encouraged to play his flute throughout the night watch, because of his special relationship to urSu. In front of urZah were three pots.

When the first pale flush of dawn light tinged the mists rising around the stones, urZah gently pushed Jen's flute away from his lips. At the same moment, urUtt struck a plangent harmony that resonated for a long time.

The next to sound was urTih the Alchemist, who used his right front arm—an artificial limb of wood, like the right leg—to make a bowl sing. It was a bowl he had fashioned from seven metals, and when he drew his wooden arm firmly around the rim, the bowl howled as though with the voice of a wandering spirit, ululating when he tipped the water inside it from side to side.

Others joined in, working to a slow pulse of rhythm. UrAc the Scribe struck a gong, urYod the Numerologist rang a passing bell, and urSol the Chanter raised his mighty voice, leading the rest in a great chorus.

Meanwhile, the touch of dawn light had activated the small crystal at the end of the Master's staff, where it lay on the central stone. First, the crystal glowed as though concentrating the light in itself. Then the wood around it smoldered and began to burn. The flame moved slowly down the stick, away from the crystal, leaving behind a line of white embers and a scorch-mark on the stone. The smoke curled into the mists, which were filling with light.

UrZah picked up one of the three pots in front of him and tipped it upside down, pouring a stream of dry soil into Jen's hand. UrUtt was playing in the lowest register of his harp, and urSol directed the chorus accordingly.

"With the ground, be one," urZah told Jen.

He threw the pot away. It shattered on the tallest Standing Stone, scattering fragments over urSu's coat.

UrZah picked up the second pot. UrUtt and urSol moved to the middle register. From the pot urZah poured water over Jen's hand.

"With water, be one."

He threw the pot after the first and picked up the third. The harp and chanting soared. When urZah upturned the pot, nothing came out.

"With the air, be one."

He handed the pot to Jen, who looked at him questioningly. UrZah offered no answer. Jen threw the pot against the stone, where it shattered. UrZah nodded slowly.

The staff had burned itself away. Its expiring smoke rose to meet a lambent wraith of mist that seemed to be descending into the triangle of stones. Jen saw that the coat of urSu had now evaporated into nothingness. Only the shards of the smashed pots remained where the coat had been.

"Be one, Jen," urZah told him, "and make one. Now you must go, as the Master told you."

"Go?" Jen asked, "Go where? What must I do?"

For years he had yearned to leave the valley. The urRu had raised him with loving care: at the appointed times they had cut his hair, taught him to swim, to tie knots, to sharpen a knife; had initiated him into the mysteries of music and the principles of geometry; had tested him by tasks and isolation—but never had they allowed him to explore outside the valley. And now that he was bidden to leave, he wished to remain, to say he was not yet ready. The truth, he realized, was that he did not want to abandon what was familiar and customary. Besides, it was one thing to wish to explore. It was quite another to be expelled.

"You must go where the Master showed you," urZah told him. "To the high hill, to the dome of Aughra, who watches the heavens and keeps her secrets."

"UrSu showed me such an image in a bowl. But I don't know where the place is. How do I get there? What am I supposed to do there? How do I know I can do it? And who is Aughra?"

UrZah replied, in his slow voice, "Your need is to go with questions, not with answers, as the cave needs the mountain."

Jen controlled a rising feeling of panic. "But urZah, you can see the future, can't you? Please at least tell me what will happen."

UrZah paused. The urRu continued their chanting as the sun rose above the rim of the horizon.

"The future is many futures," urZah told him. "We see them all. Which one will be yours is for you to seek." He pointed at a carving on the Standing Stone near them. It pictured three concentric circles inside a triangle. "This I will tell you," urZah went on. "Very soon the three made one will look down. Great vibrations will be felt by all who touch rock. Unless by then you have found the future you must seek, and made what was broken whole, what was dark light, then nothing can be whole, and dark will be the fate of all creatures on Thra."

"But I am frightened of what is dark, urZah."

"With reason," the urRu replied. "Darkness imprisons the light. Darkness destroys all beings, covets all energy. It is evil."

"What is evil?" Jen asked.

"Evil does not exist," urZah answered. "Evil is disharmony between existences. Now go, Gelfling, with your questions."

UrZah turned away, faced the sun, and joined the chanting of the urRu.

Jen took his first steps up the spiral path leading out of the valley. When he reached the cave where he had lived with urSu, he paused and looked down into the thalweg. Rising up to him came the deep, nine-toned chant of the urRu. He saw that they were all staring up at him.

Whether it was their gaze or their chant or the seed of courage he had experienced at urSu's death, he did not know, but a force propelled him past the mouth of the cave and on up the spiral path.

At the shoulder of the valley, higher than he had ever been on his own, he glanced back once more. The waterfalls were tiny, sparkling jewels in the early sunlight. He took a deep breath. For the reassurance of a familiar object in a strange world, he put his hand up to touch his flute, which he carried on a leather neck-string.

Near him was another line of Standing Stones. They were tall and narrow, shooting up from the ground like needles. Seen from the valley below, they had always marked the boundary of his world. On them he saw carvings similar to those on the stones that formed the triangle down below, where the chanting of the urRu continued, still surprisingly distinct even from where Jen stood. Perhaps, Jen thought, the carvings might offer him some indication of the direction he was supposed to take.

He approached the nearest stone to examine it. It had a black patina on it, like soot. He reached out to rub it off but withdrew his hand sharply. The stone was burning hot. He remembered what he had seen the previous day, sparks traveling across the valley and over its rim. These stones must have been struck by lightning.

He breathed deeply again and walked on, over the shoulder of the valley and out of sight of his home. After a few steps, the ground in front of him began to slope down again. Soon Jen was standing on the brink of a wide, bowl-shaped plain, lush with vegetation and sprinkled with woods. Far away, on the misty horizon, the plain terminated in a range of rounded hills.

"To the high hill," urZah had said. That must be the direction he had to take.

Brian Froud

CHAPTER II
ON AUGHRA'S HIGH HILL

The complex pattern on the ceremonial floors of the castle of the Dark Crystal represented a path. No one who saw it could doubt that. What was open to interpretation was where the path had started, where it might end, and, indeed, what the purpose of the journey might be.

With its forks and intersections, its arcs and spirals and spheres, leading from room to room, it would probably have been seen by one of a transcendentalist cast of mind as a pilgrim's path, the way of enlightenment, leading from station to station of ascending consciousness. Originating in a brute, dark matter, the traveler would, metaphorically, rise toward pure spirituality, though never in a straight progression but always circuitously, even after the journey had apparently been accomplished. (For even the purely spiritual soul has unfinished work to do. The cycle of the floor's pattern extended infinitely.)

The Skeksis, however, did not take that view. The assumption that pure spirituality was in some sense a higher form of being than brute matter was not self-evident to them. How they interpreted the pattern on the floor was clear on the day following the funeral of their Emperor.

For them it was a path to the throne.

He who aspired to clutch the scepter in his talons was well advised to be seen treading the path. It suggested some vestigial humility, a sense of due observance, a willingness to submit oneself to a proper discipline. Thus it was that three of them—the Ritual-Master, the Chamberlain, and the Garthim-Master—had spent some hours edging along the path, with the expected solemnity, while the rest of the Skeksis formed an audience. Round and round the path the three of them went. And as they went, they studied the complexities of the pattern and experimented by taking different forks, different routes always to the same end, in which was their beginning.

Each of them was hopeful that sooner or later some hitherto overlooked clue might present itself to him, some untrodden path that, by a psychic machinery he could not guess at, would yield the throne to him. How had the late deceased Emperor accomplished this? None of them could recall.

As their patience dwindled, their pace gradually increased. None of the three now left the Throne Room but studiously gyrated closer and closer to the dais and the throne itself. Their eyes were flickering around beadily. Each of them had to keep a close watch on the other two in order to forestall a sudden lunge for the throne. But there were also factions to consider among the rest of the Skeksis. Would the Treasurer and the Scroll-Keeper preserve their traditional loyalty to the Ritual-Master? Would the Garthim-Master still command the powerful support of the Scientist and the Slave-Master? And would the Chamberlain still be joined in a triple alliance with the Gourmand and the Ornamentalist— the triad that, together with the old Emperor, had formed the largest, and therefore successful, faction at the previous enthronement?

It was the Chamberlain, filled with a righteous sense of his prior claim, who finally made a grab for the scepter. Wielding it shoulder-high like a scimitar, he spun round to glare at the other two contenders, screeching and snarling his defiance. From his bared, yellow fangs saliva dripped onto the silken floor of the dais.

The Ritual-Master was outraged. This was no way to behave on such a solemn occasion. Due rite and custom had to be observed, or everything was lost. He started to make a speech of protest, a quivering talon pointed at the Chamberlain in denunciation of his gross ambition.

The Garthim-Master's reaction was different but no less vehement. Striding up to the dais, he thrust his face out at the Chamberlain so that they were fang to fang. In his deep voice, the Garthim-Master pronounced one word. "*Haakskeekah!*"

A thrill ran through the watching Skeksis.

The Chamberlain had no option. He could not now be seen to shrink from the most solemn challenge of the Skeksis. Hissing back into the Garthim-Master's face, the scepter still held high, he returned the challenge in an eldritch shriek. "*Haakskeekah!*"

At this point, the Ritual-Master withdrew from the contest. Opinion among the rest of the onlooking Skeksis differed on his motivation. Some argued that his innate sense of ceremonial propriety inhibited him. Others maintained that, not being directly challenged, he was evading the ordeal of *Haakskeekah!* And a further view was that he was making a political calculation: against the sheer strength of the Garthim-Master and the constitutional claim of the Chamberlain, he could not hope to be the victor; but by withdrawing at this stage he would assure himself the vice-regency beneath whichever of them triumphed, and thus he would be next in line to the throne.

Whatever his reasons, the Ritual-Master moved to the center of the Throne Room and took charge of the situation. He gave a nod in the direction of the watching Slave-Master, who waddled off to prepare for the ritual. The rest stood still, murmurous with eager anticipation. Many trine had passed since the trial of *Haakskeekah!* had been witnessed in that chamber.

The Slave-Master returned with a score of Pod People, whom he sent to the side of the room. There they hauled on a long rope running down from a pulley mounted high on the wall. In the middle of the floor, a slab of stone was slowly raised.

When it had cleared the surrounding floor, the Slave-Master called out a command. Having secured the rope, the slaves ran across the floor, and with their shoulders pushed the slab, which was supported on a pivot, through an arc of ninety degrees. It took them a long time, such was the dead weight of the stone. The Skeksis grinned and twitched with excitement. The Garthim-Master and the Chamberlain furtively watched each other out of the corners of their eyes. The Chamberlain had reluctantly laid the scepter back on the throne.

The Slave-Master then issued another order. The slaves ran back to the side of the room and hauled on another rope that was hanging parallel to the first. From the pit that the revolving slab had disclosed, a rock slowly emerged, finally coming to floor level. It was a remarkable rock. Six feet in height, made of granite, in origin it could have been a cromlech stone. But it had lost its gloss and pride; it was a dull, unreflective boulder, mutilated by gashed scars.

The Ritual-Master ceremoniously held out both his arms toward the Slave-Master, who strutted forward bearing two massive broadswords. The Ritual-Master bent his head over the weapons and spat on each in turn. They were then presented to the duelists. The Chamberlain, having given each of them a trial whirl around his head, chose first. The Garthim-Master took his, the Slave-Master retreated to the margin of the floor, and the Ritual-Master intoned, "*Pih Tabrokh!*"

As the one challenged, the Chamberlain had had the advantage in choice of sword. His disadvantage was that he had to strike first. He approached the rock, dragging his sword on the ground, where it made a trail of little blue sparks. Then he raised the sword to shoulder level, swung it around several times, gathering momentum, and smashed it into the rock with a defiant shout of "*Haakskeekah!*"

The sword made a dull clank on the stone. Nothing else happened except for a violent jarring of the Chamberlain's back and tepid applause from the Ornamentalist and the Gourmand.

The Garthim-Master stepped up with a derisive sneer. Grunting, then roaring, he swung the sword around once and dashed it against the rock. "*Haakskeekah!*"

A bright spark flashed and a chip of granite flew off from the impact and skittered across the floor. It was not a decisive blow, the watching Skeksis knew, but the Slave-Master and the Scientist cheered it in their guttural voices. The Treasurer and the Scroll-Keeper also croaked their admiration, in the hope that they had chosen the winning side. The Chamberlain took the applause to be a goad from his enemies. They always had underrated him. Very well then, as Emperor he would make them regret it.

This time, he wound up his momentum by spinning his whole body around, like a dervish, some yards away from the rock. Then, in a sequence of three advancing gyrations, he arrived with his sword swinging through the air. He hammered it into the rock with such awful power that it would hardly have been surprising to see the stone sliced in two. "*Haakskeekah!*" he gasped.

There was a tiny spark at the point of impact. A scintilla flew off and over the heads of the slaves, hitting the wall with an almost undetectable

Jim Henson's Creature Shop

ping. The only other sounds in the chamber were the Chamberlain's groan of pain as he held his back and ambiguous rumbles in the throats of the Ornamentalist and the Gourmand.

With a stentorian bellow of laughter, the Garthim-Master stepped forward again. Standing beside the rock, he grimaced several times, swinging his sword. He balanced ponderously back on one foot, spun himself around once, and then, leaning on his front foot, drove the blade into the rock at full arm's length. "*Haakskeekah!*" he thundered.

With a flash and boom of released energy, a white-hot chunk of rock the size of the Chamberlain's head crashed to the floor.

"*Haakskeekah!*" bayed the watching Skeksis, in praise of their new Emperor. "*Haakskeekah, Khrokon! Haakskeekah! Haakskeekah!*"

In a minstrel gallery above, an assembled choir of Pod slaves struck up with an anthem of conquest. Up and down the chamber the Garthim-Master held both hands on high, mumbling some words of benediction. At the side of the room, the slaves looked on mute and expressionless. Their eyes were milky and unfocused.

Beside the ravaged rock, the Chamberlain cowered wretchedly. He was nothing now. Worse than nothing: a magnanimous gesture to one's defeated opponent was no part of the Skeksis' tradition. At best he would be able to slink away when no one was looking and perhaps self-effacingly resume his duties as Chamberlain, since none could deny his administrative competence.

But the Garthim-Master was not so inclined. Slumped arrogantly on his throne, with the Ritual-Master kneeling before him, he affected an offhanded gesture in the direction of the rock. The rest of the Skeksis took their cue. Grinning and hissing, unsheathing their talons, they surrounded the Chamberlain. In moments they had stripped him of his insignia, badges, chains, precious gems, even his layers of mouldering robes.

In order to preserve his very skin, the Chamberlain bowed low to the ground and crept away, whimpering, out of the chamber, clad only in rags and tatters.

Now was the time of high rejoicing in the castle of the Skeksis. The choir sang on, while a silken canopy was held aloft over the Garthim-Master. "*Khrokon, Khrokon!*" the Skeksis acclaimed their new Emperor, as the Ritual-Master gravely advanced to place the crown on his majestic head. The scepter was solemnly handed to him, and he leaned forward to allow a robe of satin, trimmed with fur and winking with rubies and emeralds, to be laid over his shoulders. The Ritual-Master stepped back from the dais and made deep obeisance. "*Khrokon, Khrokon!*" rang out the loyal cries, as the remaining Skeksis also fell to their knees.

The Ritual-Master rose again and held out his hand. The Ornamentalist stepped forward with a chalice, which he handed to the Ritual-Master. It was full of freshly drawn Pod vliya, the life-juice that the Scientist extracted from captives when they were first brought into the castle, ready to be turned into slaves.

The Ritual-Master raised the chalice above his head and turned, offering it votively to the new Emperor.

The chalice slipped from his hands and hit the floor. Vliya ran in rivulets across the spiral-pattern.

"Idiot archimandrite!" the Garthim-Master snarled at him, lapsing into unceremonial demotic speech.

The Ritual-Master's mouth and eyes were opened wide. "The Crystal!" he babbled. "The Crystal!"

The Garthim-Master's jaw snapped shut. He listened, as did all the other Skeksis. In the noise of their sycophantic rejoicing, they had not until that moment heard the warning ring emanating from the great Crystal.

The Garthim-Master leaped from his throne and rushed from the room, followed by the other Skeksis. Behind them, slaves came forward emotionlessly to mop up the vliya. Their own vliya had been distilled from them upon their arrival, and out with it had flowed both feeling and thought.

Still clad in his robe and crown, and clutching his scepter like a sword, the Garthim-Master led the charge along the corridors of the castle and into the Crystal Chamber. There the eight Skeksis, talking agitatedly, gathered to see what the Crystal had relayed to the castle from the Crystal Bats that monitored the planet.

There it was. A Gelfling! The Garthim-Master thrust out a quivering talon; and the rest, looking on, fell silent.

The Garthim-Master's eyes bulged with astonishment, then outrage. "Garthim!" he screamed. "Garthim!"

In response to the summons, all around the castle, from the ceremonial chambers to the Garthim pit itself, the waiting Garthim, standing like suits of armor, came suddenly to life, with a loud ticking sound.

"A Gelfling," the Garthim-Master was bellowing, "on Aughra's high hill."

Huge black carapaces lumbered along the corridors to the tube that was the only exit from the castle. Down it they vomited forth into the world outside.

Hidden in the shadows of an alcove, the Chamberlain watched the Garthim clatter past, then crept stealthily after them.

Around the Crystal, the Skeksis muttered ominously among themselves. This was inconceivable, a Gelfling still alive. The entire race had been liquidated. Surely they could not have regenerated themselves spontaneously. Things of that sort did not happen. The Scientist was rapidly elaborating a theory of interrupted transmission: Suppose this inexplicable image in fact relayed an event that had taken place long ago and that, by some freak of physics he was not yet in a position to elucidate, was only now registering its electrical impulses on the receiving Crystal. As a theory, it left a lot to be explained. But it was more plausible than a live Gelfling, and much less unnerving to the Skeksis.

Gazing at the image deep within the Crystal's dark core, the Garthim-Master was hoarsely commanding his Garthim, "Kill it! Kill it! Kill it! Kill it!"

After leaving the valley, Jen traversed the lush green plain, heading for the range of rounded hills on the horizon. His eyes widened at the variety of small animals warily scattering upon his approach and at the exotic plants he saw. Some plants towered high above him, with smooth, curving stems and, at their tops, blossomlike pastel clouds or succulent sprays of deep-hued petals.

At first he was exhilarated to be completely alone, with the whole world before him. It was the biggest adventure of his life. After a time, with the valley of the urRu ever farther behind him, he started to feel slightly scared. If anything happened now, he was on his own, with nowhere to run, no one to turn to for protection. He eyed purple berries like those the urRu had forbidden him to eat and decided not to try them yet.

He forded a shallow stream and climbed a knoll, covered with bunches of knot-grass, to see what lay around him. If only there were creatures here to whom he could speak—Gelfling above all, but if that was too much to hope for then any being who could understand his language.

From the top of the grassy knoll he saw a shimmer of movement far ahead of him, beside the stream that wriggled across the plain. It looked like a line of shadows flickering first one way, then the other, back and forth. He walked down toward it. Coming closer, he saw that the shimmering was caused by a crowd of insects, nearly as large as himself. Each of them had ten long and sticklike legs. Their small bodies, high above the ground, were the color of silver gilt. As though obeying an invisible director, they were performing a curious dance, taking a few awkward steps together in one direction, and then all together reversing their movement.

Jen was not sure if they had registered his approach. They betrayed no sign of fear, yet the locus of their lateral movements began to edge closer to the stream, until several of them were dancing on the water itself.

A playful impulse prompted Jen to join their dance. He took up a position at the end of the line and stepped sideways with them and back again. Each time the movement was completed, he found that he was a little closer to the stream; and the moment came when he had to put one foot on the surface of the water if he was to maintain his position in the line. He did so with confidence and found that his foot, unlike theirs, broke the surface and sank into the soft, silty mud.

That appeared to alarm the insects. At once they abandoned their stately prancing. Each of them folded its ten legs together, and from its body spread a pair of deep-damasked wings, striped red and gray-green. In a pack, they buzzed up into the sky and circled above Jen, who stood, one foot in the mud, craning his neck to watch them.

They remained there, wheeling above him, until he had set forth again toward the hills. At some distance he looked behind him and saw that they had resumed their gaunt ballet.

He was a wanderer in a strange country, but a wanderer with a purpose or, at least, with a destination. What he was supposed to do when he arrived was a thought he kept suppressed during the day. But as he entered the foothills, the sight of a dome high up on a peak, glinting in the sunlight, sent a thrill of determination through him.

He knew he had made a start in the right direction. He would find the one called Aughra and hope that from her he could gather some explanation of that other vision his dying Master had shown him: the crystal shard.

As he climbed the cliff toward the dome, he noticed a bird—or was it a bat?–hovering near him. What he did not notice was that in its talons it grasped a small crystal, violet in color, in which his image was a tiny reflection.

Jen reached a cliff ledge broad enough to afford him a rest. Sitting there, he allowed himself to gaze down and compare the distance he had climbed to that which remained. It had been hard going, and risky, this climb. Although his fingers were already sore and his thighs ached with fatigue, he reckoned with disappointment that he was only just past the halfway mark. There must no doubt be an easier route up to the dome, but urZah had impressed upon him that he had no time to spare, and walking around the foothills in search of a less arduous path to the top might take days.

He tried to relax and enjoy the view. It would have pleased him to pick out, in the terrain spread beneath him, the valley of the urRu, but he found it impossible. The far side of the plain corrugated itself into a great volcanic expanse filled with valleys, craters, and ravines.

The strange bat-bird thing was still hunting the cliff. Probably it had its nest there. No other birds could be seen. That, Jen reasoned, would be because the bat-bird was their predator. The only living things he saw on the cliff were rock spiders. He was intrigued, also, to notice that the cliff was studded with outcrop crystals of all colors. Some of them were large enough to offer him a climbing hold.

Jen took a series of deep, slow breaths to relax his muscles and prepare for the final ascent. He realized he was hungry. There had been pools and streams to drink from in the plain, but he had recognized nothing that he knew for sure was edible. Perhaps the one called Aughra would turn out to be kind and offer him food.

He started to climb again. Foothold, test it, fingerhold, test it, and up. Take it easy, a small step each time, no need to hurry. Plan ahead when you can. Keep your head upright. Foothold, test it, fingerhold, test it, and up. He had some experience rock climbing among the waterfalls in the valley. There, if he fell, he would land in the pool. Here…

With a firm hold, he arched his back so that he could see the top of the cliff. The distance was deceptive, but he thought he was not far away now.

The last ten feet were sheer vertical. He put out of his mind the penalty of failure and concentrated fiercely on solving the problems of the cliff. A little fringe of grass told him just where the top was. He moved within reach, hooked his fingers over it, and with one last heave, straightening up on his arms, he was there, panting heavily.

When he had recovered, he stood up and looked around for the dome. He could not see it because the top of the cliff was not yet the top of the mountain. In front of him was a craggy mass of rocks, with shrubs and grasses growing thickly. The turf where he stood was on a path that led around the rocks and, presumably, to the top. He walked along it, following its gently rising curve.

He came to a place where the path widened, allowing room on either side for trees and vinelike creepers to grow. As he walked, he searched for fruit or nuts, but found none. To cheer himself up, he played on his flute.

Giant hanging tendrils blocked his path. As he brushed them aside, he felt himself seized around the arms. Before he could see who his assailant was, more thongs wound around him, binding him tightly, helplessly. His feet left the ground as he was carried into the air, into the leaves of the trees, and there suspended. His writhing and kicking were all in vain, since he was gripped much too closely by the snare.

He did manage to stretch his head far enough forward to see what it was that bound him. It was the tendrils. He must be their prey. Were they carnivorous?

Then he heard some animal approaching on the ground below the trees. The undergrowth crackled beneath its feet. Its breath was loud, rasping, rheumy. He could not see through the foliage to determine what it was. He ceased writhing and froze, scarcely breathing himself.

His heart almost stopped when a single eyeball emerged through the leaves and stared at him, unblinkingly. All he could do was stare back at it. Very pale blue, it was heavily bloodshot, like a broken-veined leaf.

As the initial shock diminished, he could see that the eyeball was held in a gnarled hand. Now the hand withdrew the eye, and below he heard a sound that might have been the smacking of lips.

Gradually, carefully, the tendrils lowered him down through the leaves, but not as far as the ground. He hung there, still bound fast, looking at a hag who was screwing the eyeball back into her face. When she spoke, her voice was a ruin. "You Gelfling?" she asked in his tongue.

"I am," Jen said.

She shook her head, with its lank gray mane, and loudly sucked her teeth in doubt. "Can't be. All dead. All destroyed. Long time since."

"My name is Jen." He paused for thought. "Jen the Gelfling. I have not been destroyed."

"Ha," she said. "Maybe. Maybe not."

"Are you Aughra," Jen asked, "who watches the heavens?"

"How you know about me?"

"I was sent by my master, urSu, the wisest of the urRu."

She looked around nervously. "Where's he, then? Huh? With you, is he?"

"He is dead," Jen told her.

She sniffed. "Could be anywhere, then."

Although her eye was back in place, her appearance was not less terrifying than her eyeball alone had been. She was stout, clad in a ragged, stained wine-colored tunic that smelled of strong chemicals. Her arms were like weathered walnut branches; he could not see her legs. Above her broad shoulders, unkempt hair straggled down a face that not only was hideous now but could never have been better than ugly: a broad nose with hair sprouting from the gaping nostrils; a single swiveling eye; no eyebrows above either her eye or her empty socket; and two rows of blasted black stumps for teeth. *Was* she a woman? Jen wondered. Since the long-ago day when he had lost his mother, he had never met a female of any species that could talk to him, and he was not entirely confident he knew the difference between the genders. UrSu had never been helpful in the matter when Jen had put questions to him. All he had answered was that the urRu had evolved as a species of neither gender, and that it was therefore a subject of which he had no concept. And since Jen had not known whether he would ever meet a female, he had not pressed his questions. About Aughra, there was something he could not name that struck him as what "female" would mean. And urZah, in speaking of Aughra, had said, "who watches the heavens and keeps her secrets." Yet, this voice of hers, harsh and broken and short of breath, was that the voice a female had? Well, Jen reflected, although it was a brisk voice, she did speak Gelfling, however haltingly. That gave him some reassurance that, on this mission of his, those he met might know his language.

"Can you release me from these tendrils?" he asked.

"Could do," she answered but did not move. "Where did you come from?"

"I have come from under the mountain, where I dwell with the urRu."

She reacted only by muttering, "Gelfling, hmm?" and nodding. She pinched the flesh of his arms, where they were free of the tendrils' embrace, then thrust her snout forward to sniff his body. Involuntarily, he gave a little cry of nervousness.

She cackled and seemed quite pleased. "Ha! Afraid of me, is it? Think I might eat you, huh? Nice roast Gelfling, eh? That might be tasty, yes. Ha ha."

As she laughed, she again put her eye close to Jen's face. The dank stench of her breath made him fear he would retch.

"What you want with Aughra?" she asked in a more severe tone.

Jen could think of nothing to reply but the truth. There was no point in trying to deceive her, anyway. "My Master sent me, as I told you. He showed me an image of your dome. And then he showed me another image of a shard of crystal. I do not understand completely what he was telling me I had to do, but if I can find the shard I might—"

She interrupted him. "That's all? A crystal piece you want, huh? Why not say?"

To his enormous relief, she now stroked the tendrils with a most curious gentleness. They lowered him to the ground and released him. While he was rubbing the circulation back into his limbs, she turned and started to walk up the path. "Follow," she said. "Gelfling. Ha!"

After a few yards, Aughra wheeled to her right apparently walking into the rocks. Bushes and tall grasses drew aside for her, and revealed a hole leading into the hills. She ducked inside. Jen hesitated for a moment before following her. But there was nothing else for him to do.

The hole became a tunnel through the rocks. Blinded by the

Brian Froud

thin black like ridge
decorated

Tusk

SG

thin
ridge

darkness a few steps in, Jen stumbled along, guided by the sounds of Aughra's clomping feet but afraid of crashing against the stone. Several times he called out to her to wait for him, that he could not see where he was going, but she neither answered him nor paused. With his hand outstretched before him to protect himself, Jen was dimly aware that the tunnel was a circuitous maze.

Suddenly there was a brief blaze of light ahead of him. Aughra had opened a door at the end of the tunnel and passed through it. Darkness enfolded Jen again. He blundered against the tunnel's walls, close to panic, until his hands encountered the door and pushed it open.

Inside, he stopped, dumbstruck at all he saw. He was standing beneath a vast dome that was illuminated by a golden radiance, from what source he could not tell. But more stupendous was what he beheld within the dome: an enormous and complicated orrery in constant and swift operation, modeling the relative motions and fixities of the trisolar system. Many-hued planets mounted on shafts of different lengths revolved in varying rhythms and orbits around the center, rising and falling; and around them in turn rotated moons and other satellites in their own trajectories, while eccentrically spinning comets danced in and out of the whole convoluted, interweaving, four-dimensional cosmos. Jen gaped. Never had he dreamed of anything so wonderful, so incomprehensible.

He was still staring in bewilderment when he realized that a planet as large as himself was rapidly about to sweep down on him. He threw himself flat on the floor and felt the planet pass an inch above his head. He looked around for a safer place, but the orbits of the orrery seemed to encompass the great room.

Where was Aughra? Clearly this was where she lived, as well as her place of work. Her domestic clutter, pots and pans and utensils and glassware, lay scattered around, amidst alchemists' tools, biological specimens, and bits and pieces of half-assembled machines. He raised his eyes and saw a gallery running the circumference of the dome, with two large telescopes mounted diametrically opposite each other. But he could not see her up there, either.

"Like my house, eh, Gelfling?"

Jen jumped. Aughra had suddenly appeared behind him, perhaps emerging from some trapdoor.

"Such marvels," Jen said. "I never knew–"

"Ha! What you expect, huh? Hole in ground?" She grunted. "Gelfling."

Aughra ducked casually as an urgent, spiked moon slashed past her gray head with the whoosh of a battle-ax. Jen, with his back to it, had not seen it coming. A foot lower and it would have decapitated him.

"Where should I stand that is safe?" he asked her.

"Safe?" she snorted. "You won't find safe here. Nor anywhere. Just watch out. Get used to it soon enough, when you know what to expect."

Jen nodded at the orrery. "What is that?"

"It tells you what to expect. Like now you're going to lose an arm if you don't look around."

Jen looked around quickly, just in time to dodge a bright comet. "But–" he started.

"Follow," Aughra told him, laughing to herself. She led him halfway around the room to a niche that was presumably a sanctuary from the dangerous cosmos. There she sat him down at a table. "You hungry?" she asked.

"Yes." Jen had forgotten that he was. Too much was happening too quickly.

She opened a cupboard door, and gave him a piece of cheese and a beaker of white juice. He sniffed them cautiously.

"Go on," Aughra said. "Do no harm to the Gelfling. Used to eat that all the time. Nebrie cheese. Kainz juice. What *you* eat, then? You really Gelfling?"

"Yes," Jen said hurriedly. "Tell me, you used to know other Gelfling, you said?"

"Maybe." It was disconcerting how abruptly Aughra could become taciturn.

"But you said—"

"I said lots of things. Too many. Nobody to talk to, that's why."

"I would like to know more about the other Gelfling. I've never met one."

"Never will. All dead. Skeksis sent Garthim." She stared at him, shaking her head in puzzlement. "Go on, eat."

Jen took a bite of the cheese. It tasted good. He sipped the juice and found it delicious. All the time, Aughra was shamelessly staring at him.

"Excuse me," Jen said, "but would you tell me something? Are you female?"

Aughra laughed out loud. It was not an attractive thing to see, with her black teeth and squat body, but it cheered Jen up. "Female," she chuckled, "yes, bit that lasts is female. Bit gone rotten is male. Too busy. Oh-ho."

"What happened to your eye?" Jen asked with more confidence. "The one you can't take out, I mean."

"Eye? Burned out."

Jen gasped. "How horrible."

"Worth it." She tapped the empty socket. "I saw Great Conjunction. I saw what Crystal did. Only one, me. No one else saw it." She leaned her face close to Jen, who stopped chewing his Nebrie cheese. "*I looked at Crystal,*" she declared with emphatic satisfaction.

Jen nodded as though he understood a word of it all, and went on chewing. It really was good, this cheese.

"Only one, me," Aughra repeated. "Except urSkeks, of course. Ha! They're different, so. When they set up that chant, out here, everywhere, reverberating crystals were, then, all over Thra. Did you know?"

Jen decided that he did not know that and shook his head.

"No. I thought not. Well, that's why Aughra built this, see? They helped, before Great Conjunction, last one." She gestured to the orrery. "What you think it is all for, huh?"

"To tell you what to expect?" Jen suggested.

"How you know that, Gelfling?" she asked suspiciously.

"You told me."

"Ah. I did. Well, how else you or Skeksis or anyone know about conjunctions without all this? Hmmmm?" She leaned forward again and spoke intently. "How else you know about Great Conjunction coming? That's why you here, no? Aughra knows."

"My Master told me something about it."

"How *he* know?" Aughra asked sharply.

"I can't say. He was dying and didn't answer my questions. What is the Great Conjunction?"

Aughra gave a deep chuckle. She leaned across to a workbench and picked up an alchemist's brass triangulum. With her other hand, she took out her eyeball and held it so that it was staring at Jen through the triangulum. "See?" she asked. "Three circles. All together. Concentric, huh? Three sun brothers. Big quarrel over daughter of moon. That's story they tell, you ask Pod People. They need stories, them. She drowns herself, they separate, and when they come together again, *zzzah!*" Aughra hammered the triangulum on the table, making little rings on the surface of the white juice. "Big battle. Or big friendship. Can't tell."

"I see," Jen said. "Could we look for that shard of crystal now?"

"Wait, Gelfling," Aughra replied, screwing her eyeball back in. She replaced the brass triangulum on her workbench and wandered around the table where Jen sat. She peered into boxes and opened drawers, still talking. "You want to know about Great Conjunction. When it do come, you better be underground. No telling. End of world, maybe. Or beginning. End, beginning, all the same. Big change. Good, bad, I don't know. Whole planet might burn up. End of Thra. End of Aughra…*fffft*. You too. Smoke rings. So? We all turn to smoke one day, no? Come from smoke too, some say. Don't know. Might not be so bad, smoke. Float around. In air. See world. Hmmmm?" Suddenly she laughed hysterically.

Jen smiled, out of politeness.

Now she was talking intently to him again. "Only one, me, who really knows. Three times three ages, I watch, lesser conjunctions, some energy there, yes. But not enough. Nothing's changed, can't be. What's coming now, ah. But you see little moon, there?" She pointed to the orrery.

Jen's eyes followed the line of her bony finger and saw a very small, dark-painted orb rotating around one of the largest of the planets.

"Secret moon of Thra, that," Aughra told him with a nod. "Nobody really knows if it there. Doesn't reflect, see? *If* it there, it gravity has, yes, and that changes everything else, see? *Everything else*," she repeated. "Maybe. Maybe not. Could be soon, or not at all."

Jen remarked, "UrZah told me something would happen shortly."

Aughra smiled nonchalantly. "Suns might miss each other." She tapped her nose. "But I know. Guess how?"

Jen thought and pointed to the orrery. "That tells you?"

"Idiot. Gelfling. I just *told* you, could be error in gravity calculation on that. No. I tell you. Lots of crystals now. All over ground. Everywhere

I go. That always tells you, great metamorphosis due. I saw it last time, when Skeksis came."

Jen frowned. He had heard that word from his Master and more than once now from Aughra. "Skeksis?" he asked. "What are Skeksis?"

Aughra sat down and gazed at him in silence for a long time. With incredulity she finally answered, "You don't know that? What you doing here?"

"I told you. A shard."

"And what you want shard for?" She glowered at him.

Jen felt stupid. "I don't know yet."

Aughra spoke vehemently. "Better find out fast, Gelfling."

"Perhaps you could tell me?"

She hesitated and seemed ill at ease. "I don't know," she replied. "I don't know. Skeksis…" She shrugged.

"Are they something you're frightened of?"

She snickered. "You think Aughra is an idiot? Of course Aughra frightened of them."

"My Master said something about them. I think he said they had great power and shattered the sky when he was born. And they are evil, he said, but what does that mean?"

"You have seen castle?" Aughra asked.

Jen had no idea what she was talking about, but he nodded, to avert her scorn.

"That's Skeksis. They built it, them. Was a mountain, Crystal was inside mountain, down a shaft, in a cave, old cave, with a floor. That's where I *was*, on the floor, spirals I remember, when I *saw* it. Lost this." She tapped her empty socket again. "Then they came, after Great Conjunction done, they cut castle out of mountain rock. They do things there." She shook her head.

"What kinds of things?"

Aughra shook her head again and mumbled to herself. She shot a sidelong glance at Jen. "I don't know," she said. "I thought Gelfling *knew* all this."

"Perhaps the others you met did. I've never seen another Gelfling in my life. Well, not since I was very little, anyway, too little to learn anything about Skeksis or Great Conjunctions or–"

"UrRu," Aughra interrupted him. "They not tell you anything?"

"Oh, many things. But not about all this."

"But they sent you here, you said?"

"Yes."

"Because of prophecy?"

"What prophecy?"

She shook her head quite vigorously. "Don't know, don't know, don't know," she muttered to herself. "UrRu, no use, them, no use to anybody."

Jen was offended. "They are very kind," he said boldly. "They loved me and cared for me."

Aughra looked at him, her face doubtful. "Loving. Caring. That don't destroy a Skeksis."

"What?" Jen gasped with horror. "Destroy how?"

She hunched her broad shoulders and said nothing, shaking her gray head very slowly.

To pass the uneasy silence, Jen paid attention to a small retort that was suspended over a burner at the end of the table. He peered at it. Inside the glass, an indigo liquid was bubbling viscously. While he looked, however, his mind was on other things. If he had hoped that Aughra would clarify his quest, the truth was that she merely added to his confusion. And frightened him as well. Before, he had been simply anxious to discover what was expected of him, and whether he would be able to perform the task. Now, from her enigmatic silence, he guessed that his mission, whatever it was, would place him in mortal danger. And beneath her silence, he had to confess that he detected her scorn at how little the urRu had imparted to him about it all. He resented being made to feel ungrateful to them.

Miserable with doubts, he tried again. He had nothing to lose. "Aughra," he said, "these Skeksis—must they be killed?" To keep the question as casual as he could, he put his hand out toward the retort, pretending to be curious about it.

Aughra's response terrified him. She slammed her hand down on Jen's, pinning it to the table. "Don't touch!" she screamed.

"I'm sorry," Jen stammered. "I just wondered what it was."

"Questions," Aughra growled at him. "Too many questions, Gelfling. What you want, a shard? Find it."

She stepped across to a cabinet and threw open the door, disclosing a shelf full of crystalline shards, glittering at him.

Jen gaped. "Which one?" he asked.

"If Aughra knew that, wouldn't need Gelfling."

As evening darkened into night, Jen sat cross-legged on the table, examining Aughra's crystals. He had spent a long time sorting them into two piles. The larger contained those crystals he had rejected; the smaller was of those that bore some resemblance to the dagger shape his Master had shown him in the cloudy image. Aughra had left him to his task.

It came down to three crystal shards, in the end. Jen could not see how to choose among them, since they appeared to be identical— dagger-shaped, clear, all slightly flawed by internal cracks. He held them up to the light, he sounded them by knocking them on the table, he tasted them. No difference was perceptible. Even had he known for what purpose he wanted the shard, he could not have selected any one of the crystals over the other two. Perhaps Aughra would allow him to have all three. She did not seem possessive about them.

Aughra returned with a basket. "You want mushrooms?" she asked. "Caught them myself." Her temper had improved again.

"No, thank you." Jen showed her the three crystal shards. "These are all similar to the one I am seeking."

"So which is it?"

"I don't know. They seem the same."

"Must choose."

"Could I have all three?"

"Bad habit, that. No. Choose. All life is choosing."

"But you want me to be sure I have the right one, don't you? You said you needed me to do that."

"Maybe. Gelfling, huh!" She snickered. "You not first one, you know, coming here for shard. Seen plenty, I have. And, you know? Not one ever knew which. Huh!"

"So they never did find it?" Jen asked.

"Look at world. Of course"—Aughra mimicked him—"they never did find it. Lots to choose from, always have been. These outcrop crystals now, entire ones, new that is. But shards. You know what I think? Skeksis scatter them all over place so right one don't get found."

"What happened to those other Gelfling who came here?" Jen asked. "Could you tell me where they went?"

"That's easy. They went *fffft!* Skeksis picked them up on spy crystal, sent Garthim…" She ended with a shrug.

"Garthim?" Jen asked.

"That's right. Tell you a thing, shard you want is indestructible one.

But that don't help." She cackled. "Try hammer on destructible one! Ah-hah!"

"How about fire?" Jen suggested. "Or, or…" He looked around. "You must have things here. Chemicals."

"Breaking only test. That's how shard was made, don't you know that? Don't you know *anything?* When Skeksis hit big Crystal—*Kakoi* they call doing that—bang, cracks, and bits, but this shard flies off, huh? Oh, such noise! Tone-deaf, Skeksis went then, that time. I think that sound still going on in castle. Must be. Too big to decay. On and on."

As Jen gazed at the three shards an idea began to form. Aughra's talk about the sound of the crystal had reminded him of the high-pitched, double notes that had resounded in urSu's cave as the image of the shard was disappearing.

He lifted his flute to his lips. Aughra peered at it. "UrRu token, that firca," she remarked, "if I know."

Jen blew the notes he remembered. They hung shrill in the air for a long time, under the dome. And then, like an overtone, the same sound raised an octave became audible. It was a very pure sound.

Aughra looked around, not sure what was going on, watching the ringing dome, beneath which the orrery continued to rotate its spheres. When she glanced back at Jen, he was bent over one of the shards, listening to it with a rapt expression. Then he looked at it. Unmistakably, it was glinting, catching the light in a vibrant, glowing twinkle. Jen picked it up and stared into it. He was fascinated by the infinity of refractions, turning it in his hand.

Aughra was watching him. She rubbed her hands and cackled. "So that's it, Gelfling."

"Yes," Jen said, still staring into the shard. "It's beautiful. I wonder what I'm supposed to do with it now."

"Give it to me," she said, holding out her knotted hand.

Jen held the shard to his breast, protectively. "You said I could have it."

"Don't know," Aughra said, "don't know." She was shaking her head anxiously. "Give to me. Let me see. Long time I've wanted to know which one." She thrust out her hand again.

"But–" Jen started to say, with some animosity.

Jen was interrupted by a loud clicking sound. Then suddenly the wall on the far side of the observatory crashed in. Through the gap monstrous Garthim swarmed, nine or ten of them. They advanced in a straight line, smashing aside benches of glassware, chairs, bits of the orrery, anything that lay in their path. The straight line they chose led to Jen.

An old horror buried deep within him stirred. Petrified, he watched the gigantic black invaders smash their way toward him.

He might have remained there until the end had his mesmerized attention not been distracted by Aughra. Screaming, she had furiously scurried across, in front of the Garthim, trying to save her precious belongings. "No!" she howled desperately. "No, no! Out, Garthim, out of my house, out! No!" She threw a frenzied glance over her shoulder at Jen. "It's you, Gelfling. Let spy crystal see you, didn't you? Oh," she moaned.

The Garthim took no notice of Aughra. They advanced past her, knocking her over.

Jen, his wits returning, leaped to his feet and onto the table. He stuffed the shard into his tunic. Behind him was only the wall. He could not save himself by hiding in a cupboard. In front of him were the Garthim.

The cosmic cycle of the orrery was moving more swiftly, having lost pieces to the Garthim, and a planet was approaching Jen, on the long arc of its trajectory.

Jen waited. The Garthim were a few yards from him now. The

planet swung closer, but it was starting to rise in its orbit. By the time it reached him, it would be too high for him to grasp it. He did the only thing that was left to him. He ran along the table toward the oncoming planet and, jumping into the air, wrapped his arms around the shaft on which the planet was extended. Garthim claws snapped just below his boots.

The planet carried him up and around, toward the dome of the observatory, over the heads of the Garthim. Behind him, the Garthim had upset the table with its pile of shards. The small retort that had been bubbling there fell to the ground. The viscous liquid in it spilled onto the floor and at once began to burn fiercely. The table caught fire, and the flames began to spread.

As he swung around, Jen saw Aughra below him, standing with her hands to her head, weeping and cursing. "My house," she wailed, "my house." He saw her pick up an astrolabe and hurl it vindictively at the Garthim.

The planet was moving rapidly, but Jen had no fear other than of the black crustaceans below. They were swiveling around to watch him, some of them standing in the flames, which seemed not to touch them. He would soon be orbiting back down to them.

At the farthest point of its trajectory, the planet passed by the high telescope gallery under the dome itself. Hanging on to the shaft, Jen swung his legs in readiness; then he propelled himself through the air and onto the gallery.

The combined velocity of his jump and the forward motion of the shaft destroyed any chance Jen had of landing steadily on his feet, and he was hurled against the wall of the dome.

The wall cracked open. Whatever material had been used to construct the dome was as brittle as an eggshell. Jen crashed through the wall and fell out of the Observatory, into the air. His momentum took him on, clear of the dome, and landed him on a hillside sloping steeply away. Terrified, with no control over his body, Jen rolled head over heels down the hill. He landed in a bush far below the Observatory, shuddering.

It was some moments before the power to move his limbs returned to him. When it did, he moved them gingerly, in case they were no longer working. He winced with bruises but wept with relief to find that he was still alive, could still walk. Gradually he caught his breath.

Above him he heard an explosion. He jerked his head in its direction and saw the entire dome go up in flames against the night sky. Above the roar of the fire and the clatter of smashing objects, he could make out Aughra's high-pitched screaming.

"Oh, Aughra!" Jen cried out in sympathy.

He put his hand up to his breast. At least the crystal was still inside his tunic. His flute, too, had survived the ordeal.

He turned away from the hill and fled headlong into the darkness.

Far away, from across a deep ravine, Jen's flight was observed by a scaly monster of primeval appearance, decked in rags. The Chamberlain glanced back at the distant Observatory. Against the blaze he could see the Garthim silhouetted. He turned and started to force his unwieldy body through the thick, jungly brush, taking the same direction as Jen had, into the wilderness.

CHAPTER III
WITH SO MANY QUESTIONS

As soon as Jen had left the valley and the funeral rites for urSu had been completed, the urRu commenced another ritual ceremony. Indeed, the new ceremony was effectively a continuation of the funeral.

UrSol the Chanter sounded a new, more staccato theme, which the rest took up as they moved out across the thalweg, under the rising suns. UrAc the Scribe fetched prepared pots of natural-colored sand; and, near the tallest of the Standing Stones, he spread it out over a circular area of which the radius was his own body length. He smoothed the sand over with a weaving batten.

Meanwhile, the others staked out the valley floor with long lines of string, carefully measured and reckoned for intersections. All the strings crossed urAc's sand circle and were plucked in turn, making both a sound and an indentation in the sand. The sound was incorporated into the chant. Each indentation urAc filled with turquoise-colored sand. As he worked, he never ceased to chant, and what he chanted was a narrative. He described the journey of a hero.

UrAc had sand of four other colors: white, red, black, and a creamy, iridescent mother-of-pearl. He now began to use them to create his sand painting. The general form of the picture was a spiral, but across it urAc created long arcs, and at its head the icon of three concentric circles in a triangle. Along the journey of the spiral he represented some events with objects: a bird's wing, an insect's claw, a horn, a tooth, a burnt stick. He depicted twins, flames, and Jen's flute. He added a number of symbols, such as the pentacle, the tetraktys, and the double helix. All the time he chanted, with the other urRu, while the suns crossed the sky and the three shadows of the Standing Stones began to converge, encroaching on the sand painting. Layer upon layer of description, prayer, anecdote, and song were laid down.

Toward the end of the day, urAc completed his work by placing bowls of water here and there, laying out small pebbles with holes in them, and, at the intersections, inserting prayer sticks. As the three shadows crept closer to their point of conjunction, at the head of the sand painting, the Scribe finally drew in wavy, fiery lines of energy around the icon of the Great Conjunction. Now the sand painting was a thing alive. The power of conceptual thought that urAc had poured into his work had to be consummated very quickly before it dispersed.

The three shadows met, touching the icon. UrAc stood erect on his heavy hind legs and uttered a great cry. It was a cry of end and of beginning. As it was echoed by the rest of the urRu, around the valley, urAc obliterated the sand painting with one great sweep of his tail.

Facing the suns low on the horizon, the urRu set up a full-throated nine-tone diapason. All the rocks and stones of the valley rang to it.

Having escaped the evil claws of the Garthim, Jen was alone again. Through darkness, through wilderness, he had staggered away from the blazing Observatory until he reached marsh ground, where trees offered a kind of sanctuary from the dangerous world he had entered.

He wished he were back with the urRu, playing in the waterfalls. He had been at peace, there—one with the valley and with them. Everything had been in its place, harmonious. Now, it seemed as though all that life had been a sleep, a forgetting. Expelled into knowledge of the world, he did not like it much. He feared that all his acts would prove to be widows of the dreams he had once had. He felt himself to be vulnerable, piecemeal.

It was good to test oneself, and climbing the cliff had been a good test. Never again would he see anything as wonderful as what lay beneath Aughra's dome. But the dread, the black Garthim, the doubts that Aughra had put into him, all that had fractured the soul he had carried intact within him from the valley.

He was haunted by what he had seen of the Garthim. It was as though he had known them before, in nightmares. Had Aughra summoned them? he wondered. Certainly she had not wished them to destroy her Observatory, but perhaps she had expected them to attack Jen only. Then there was the question of the shard. Would she have let him take the shard away? And she had been frightened of the Skeksis, from whom, she had said, the Garthim were sent. Should he be frightened of them, too?

He had so many questions, and no one to offer him answers.

He had the shard, and no idea what to do with it.

As the dawn light tinged the sky, one question preoccupied him most. Where should he go from here? If he walked farther into the swamp, he might never get out again. And yet, he dared not turn back. Would the Garthim pursue him forever? Would they drown in the bogs of this swamp? They had been untouched by fire.

The light of day disclosed a fantastic swamp world to him. Trees trundled through the mud. Mushrooms spread gorgeous wings and whirred into flight. A fluttering butterfly was devoured by a long orange tongue flicked out from a drab stump of cactus. Puddles of liquid with a metallic sheen oozed from hollow to hollow by their own volition. It was like a laboratory in which forms of evolution were permuted. Jen saw hornets made of diamond deliver an appallingly ferocious attack on a serpent with a weasel's face. They drove it into a hole in the swamp, which snapped shut. He concluded that some buried monster employed the hornets as a hunting pack, but for what commensurate reward? A bunch of flame-colored flowers hid their attractive heads from a bee by plunging themselves into the mire. For a period, shortly after sunrise, the air seemed to be charged with radiation that caused a static, crackling noise. While it lasted, certain creatures basked in it—silver worms, ginger wading-birds, animated thin sheets of something like creamy paper, and a clutch of small, furry, eight-legged animals huddling close together. Others disappeared during the crackling radiation, presumably having withdrawn into their lairs for self-protection. Everywhere, from branches, a hairy fungus swayed, palpitating, now and then exuding a pustule that popped and left dust floating down in the still air.

Nothing here seemed to be gentle. The chain of predation was rapid and unnervingly candid. It was obvious to Jen that he would soon meet something that would seek to destroy him, even if he eluded the Garthim. Nothing here could enjoy a long life. It was all too vivid. It was visibly decomposing.

And yet, he was too exhausted to go on and too frightened to return to the open country. He had to rest. If the Garthim caught up with him here, so be it. The urRu had taught him to look upon life—his life, like all other lives—as a cycle of fate.

He sat down on a tree stump, trusting that it would remain inanimate, and took out the crystal shard. He was entranced, not only by its refractions but by something else—the suggestion of some greater power it held, some higher intelligence stored in it. Certainly this mineral object possessed a property by which the vibrations of noise and of light were united. That he knew by the glow it had given off in response to his flute.

For a long while he gazed at the shard, all the time wondering where he should go from there. The Skeksis, a Great Conjunction, evil, the three suns, a Crystal, fate, "make it whole," "heal the wound at the core of being"—all these were words he had heard said, but to him they were words without a syntax, without a dynamic relationship to each other. He was, he realized, in an even more precarious situation now than he had been in when he left the valley. Then, at least, he had a destination: the high hill. Now he simply had the shard and a nagging suspicion that, sooner or later, his journey's end would be that castle of which Aughra had spoken. "They do things there," she had said. A premonition filled him with deathly fear.

Would the shard glow again? he wondered. He put it beside him on the stump, lifted his flute to his lips, and played the notes. The shard again glowed, quite softly, and again it returned the notes raised by an octave, though with a less piercing ring than it had given under Aughra's dome. But staring into it as it lay on the stump, Jen noticed something else.

An image formed inside the shard, as the images had formed themselves in urSu's bowl. But this was a different image. Within the crystal he saw another crystal, glowing even more brightly than the first. He thought perhaps it was a refractive trick of the light. But then an event was enacted in the image: the inner crystal appeared to suffer a great blow. The prismatic pattern of its light was shattered all over the shard. The high-pitched resonance ceased and the image of the inner crystal turned dark. Then it faded. Jen was left blinking, unsure whether he had seen it all or not.

He recalled Aughra's tale of the shard—how it had broken off, with a great noise, from the large Crystal the Skeksis had hammered. If his eyes were not playing tricks on him, that must be the event that this shard had the power to shadow forth when he sounded the notes that urSu had conjured up. He felt sure it was a clue to what was expected of him.

He returned the shard to its place of safekeeping inside his tunic and lay down flat on the stump, his eyes closed. He intended to concentrate on the information he had, hoping that he might decipher a pattern there, a guide for his journey…

The next thing he knew, he was suddenly awake. He sat upright, with no idea of how long he had been asleep. He puzzled over what it was that had awakened him. A strange noise in the swamp? Or just the strong sense he had of being watched? He looked around nervously. Perhaps the noise, or the uneasy feeling, had been part of a dream in his fearful body.

As his eyes darted about, he caught a glimpse of what had been an opening in a clump of ferns snapping shut. He rose and cautiously parted the ferns, edged his head through, and looked around. No creature was there.

Then he noticed something on the ground. In the mire there was a print, slowly filling with a trickle of muddy water. As he watched, water filled and obliterated it.

Jen withdrew his head and again peered keenly around him. There were many clumps of ferns, rushes, and swamp-rooted trees behind which a creature might be lurking. Then he detected another flash of movement behind another clump of ferns, and this time he distinctly heard the sound of something scuttling away from his gaze. From the sound of it and the size of its print, it could not be anything very large. Feeling bolder, Jen moved as quickly as he could through the mire to the place where he had glimpsed the animal.

Again there was no creature to be seen, but there was a spoor. It led to a patch of firmer ground, where toadstools grew thickly. Through the toadstools, a trail of broken caps pointed directly to the open end of a fallen, hollow trunk.

Stealthily, Jen circled around to the farther end of the trunk and crouched beside it. From somewhere he heard a sound much like his own laughter. His body tensed as he looked about uneasily. The swamp was full of noises.

He leaned forward around the end of the trunk. Staring out at him was a monstrous face covered with fur. It was uttering a low, very menacing growl. Then it opened its mouth, revealing several rows of teeth, and let out an enormous, terrible roar.

Jen jumped so violently that he staggered backward. Losing his foothold on the slippery ground he fell, and landed sitting in a boggy patch. Neither his hands nor his feet could find a purchase he could use to haul himself out of the mire.

Again he heard laughter, this time behind his shoulder. He craned his neck around. From behind a tree, a Gelfling girl stepped out. She looked at him with a broad smile and laughed again.

Jen was aware of the ridiculousness of his position, but he was much too stunned by the girl's appearance to improve his dignity or to care that she was laughing at him or to feel anything at all except amazement. His open mouth made him still more a figure of fun.

Brian Froud

From the hollow log, the fierce growls continued, interspersed with yaps. Jen glanced anxiously in the direction of the furry monster.

The girl followed his glance, then gave a whistle. From the log, the face with bared teeth skipped out, revealing that it was virtually nothing but face. Its body was a tiny ball of fur, nothing more.

"Don't be afraid of Fizzgig," the girl told Jen. "He won't hurt you. He's a terrible coward." She looked at Fizzgig, who was scurrying across to hide behind her. "Aren't you?" she asked affectionately.

Fizzgig looked up at her with devotion.

The girl was the most beautiful thing Jen had seen in his life: beautiful in herself, and beautiful in existing at all. Her hair was longer and fairer than his, her eyes were larger, and the tunic she wore was brown while his was a pale, creamy color: but there was no doubt what race she belonged to—the same wide cheekbones as Jen's, the small chin, the pointed ears. When he found his voice, he said, "You are Gelfling."

"Yes," she answered.

"But…" Jen shook his head. "I thought I was the only one."

"So did I." They smiled at each other, astounded, delighted.

"I have been hidden all my life in a village near here," she said. "I live with the Pod People. My name is Kira."

"I have lived in a valley with the urRu," Jen told her, "a long way from here. I am called Jen."

He tried to stand up but found he had settled more deeply into the bog. His movements caused another round of growling from Fizzgig.

"I seem to be stuck," Jen said.

"Here," Kira said, "take my hand." She knelt down at the edge of the mire and reached out to him.

As Jen's hand touched hers, something like an electric charge was exchanged between them, and simultaneously their minds were welded into a single consciousness. A torrent of images gave each of them a clear insight into the other's innermost thoughts and memories. It was intoxicating, liberating, yet controlled, articulated like conversation, not random, gushing. The images were exchanged and shared. Jen's recollection of himself as a baby (seen more clearly now than ever before in his memories), crying amid the flaming ruins of his house, and in the distance black Garthim (as he now knew them to be) disappearing. For this Kira returned her own self image as a Gelfling infant. Swaddled, she was wedged into a hole under the roots of a tree by her mother; hidden there, she saw her mother turn away, saw a huge pair of bony, taloned hands seize her mother and strangle the life out of her, and against a background of this desolate vision saw the Garthim, again smashing, destroying, killing, wasting.

Not only were these images transmitted: both Jen and Kira had the knowledge that each was receiving the other's image exactly as though the exchange were taking place at the level of speech, where one would describe and see the other listen, respond, and acknowledge. And yet not a word was spoken between them. Only their clasped hands communicated.

Jen was gently gathered from the ruins of his house by the four arms of an urRu. Kira crawled on all fours through undergrowth and was found by a lumpish peasant man who carried her into a settlement of his people. There, she was surrounded by the community, who babbled with wonder and pleasure.

Jen, growing, splashed in the waterfalls, learned to draw runes on a black rock, and was patiently corrected by urSu. Kira swung in a hammock, was fed from a gourd, and when she jumped from a high tree provoked gasps of alarm among the peasant folk.

In a cave, Jen helped urNol mix herbs and fungi in a cauldron, which to Jen, seemed vast. UrUtt wove a garment and showed Jen how to work the loom. Under urYod's tutelage, Jen used an octonary abacus; and, cupped in the palm of urSol's hand, he studied the fingering of his flute. Kira examined plants, played cat's cradle with peasant children, of an evening sang the people's songs with them, and once hid among swamp plants while a phalanx of Garthim trooped past.

And more. Three of the urRu—urIm the Healer, urAc the Scribe, and urTih the Alchemist—taught Jen to pronounce the secret, sacred names—*Teth, Cheth, Zayin, Ab,* and so on—and used riddles to impress upon him the symbolism of pentagram and tetraktys, sulfur and quicksilver, while urAmaj and the others at first intrigued him with their obsession to connect one thing to another, and later wearied him with it. In Kira's image, her foster mother, Ydra, taught her Gelfling speech, explaining that their two races had always lived together in courteous harmony, as they had with nature. From Ydra she learned to communicate with animals and to understand the nature of plants. What neither Ydra nor any other of the peasants explained to her very well was history, especially Gelfling history. Being so deeply rooted in the life of nature, their notion of time was largely founded upon the cycle of the seasons, and barely did they comprehend the concepts of a changing world or a hungering spirit.

UrZah taught Jen to listen.

The flow of images ceased abruptly. Jen, sinking ever deeper backward into the bog, had let go of Kira's hand in his struggle to remain on the surface. The mire was up to his chin. He looked anxiously to Kira.

"It's all right," she said. "Don't struggle."

She held her head back and called out in a high-pitched wailing voice.

From deep in the mud, her call was answered by a low, rumbling noise. Looking around anxiously, Jen saw a roiling on the surface rapidly churning toward him. He hardly had time to panic before he felt himself being lifted above the mud and borne in precarious stateliness to firm ground, where he was deposited. Picking himself up, he saw what it was that had retrieved him—a grublike thing, three or four times his size. Kira was patting it affectionately on the muzzle and speaking to it in its own tongue.

Then she led Jen to a pool of clear water and helped him to wash off the mud.

"How did we tell each other so much without talking?" Jen asked her.

"Dreamfasting," Kira answered in a matter-of-fact voice, sluicing water over him with her cupped hands. Seeing that he did not understand, she asked, "You don't know about dreamfasting?"

He shook his head.

"Well…" she began, as though about to explain. Then she smiled and shrugged her shoulders. "Well, now you do know about it."

"Have you always known?"

"All my life I think, yes," Kira replied. "The Pod People know too. They're the peasant folks who raised me. Didn't your protectors use it?"

"The urRu? No. Not with me, at any rate. Can you do it whenever you want?"

In reply Kira held out her hand to him. From near their feet came a growl. "Fizzgig, don't be jealous," Kira reassured him. "This is Jen. He's like me, it seems."

She led Jen along a tree-shaded path that ran through the swamplands. He noticed the way she walked: like himself, it seemed, except that there was something in her step that was both graceful and more confident. On their way, they passed by many creatures and plants that were quite new to Jen. One grazing animal in particular was to be seen in many places, the same kind of grub as the one that had retrieved him from the bog. They were Nebrie, Kira told him, amphibious creatures the Pod People domesticated for collecting milk. When a Nebrie died, its skin was used to make drums, and the patches of fur around its face and ears were fashioned into clothes for the little Podlings.

Jen remembered that Aughra had served him Nebrie cheese, which had been delicious. He would have to explain to Kira about Aughra and the shard and the Skeksis and everything else. He could do so in dreamfasting, he hoped.

Fizzgig bravely growled at the harmless Nebrie. When they raised their grazing heads and gave him a mild glance, he bounced along the path again, following Kira and Jen.

In the banqueting hall of the castle of the Dark Crystal, seven Skeksis were seated at a long table, gorging themselves. Not sharing in the feast were the Chamberlain, who had been absent since his disgrace and the Ritual-Master, who, with an ascetic calm, sat observing the rest.

From his elaborately carved imperial chair, the Garthim-Master shot glances at the Ritual-Master beside him. What was he up to? the Garthim-Master wondered. Was this some kind of saintly, abstemious pose designed to impress the others with his holiness and so establish his right to usurp the throne at the first opportunity? The Garthim-Master regarded the others and reckoned that, if that were so, it would be a fruitless undertaking. Force, greed, and ruthlessness were the qualities the Skeksis respected in a ruler. The Garthim-Master stretched out his arm and grabbed a nearly empty cauldron from the Treasurer. He stuck his head inside it to lick it clean, then tossed it away. He kept an eye on the Ritual-Master's face and fancied he detected a flicker of distaste there. Good. That gave him an opening. Perhaps he should devise stratagems for defaming the Ritual-Master's reputation for dignity, his alleged mastery of ceremonial order. The sooner that sanctimonious creature followed the Chamberlain into the wilderness, the more secure the Garthim-Master would feel on the throne.

Slaves carried in a platter on which a freshly roasted Nebrie was steaming. The seven Skeksis set to, ducking and twisting their heads to rip off the most succulent shreds of flesh from the carcass. Again, the Ritual-Master was content to survey his carnivorous brethren.

A small, hairy-legged shellfish, renegade from a previous dish, came out of hiding and made a run for it down the length of the table. Pandemonium broke out as the Skeksis flailed the table with their talons in pursuit of the morsel. The Gourmand prevailed, popping it whole into his mouth and crunching it with a smile of relish.

With a great clatter, a troop of Garthim entered the banqueting hall, and waited in a huddle. One of them carried a bulging, wriggling sack.

The Garthim-Master wiped his mouth and looked upon the sack with satisfaction. From the size of it, his Garthim had captured not only the Gelfling but a few Pod slaves as well. They would be welcome. His newly acquired position of supreme power, the Garthim-Master felt, demanded that he have a plentiful supply of vliya, which would sharpen his decisiveness. And besides, he reasoned, what was the point of aspiring to be Emperor if he did not avail himself of all the benefits of office? The old Emperor had never stinted himself. It was watching him quaff beakers of vliya that had convinced the Garthim-Master he must be the successor. The taste of power, indeed.

"*Ekdideothone.*" The Garthim-Master commanded the Garthim to release the sack. They did so, dropping it heavily onto the marble floor.

From it, snarling and cursing her captors, Aughra emerged. She blinked her eye in the bright torchlight of the hall and rubbed her bruises angrily. "Fools!" she spat. "Skeksis, you fools! *Katakontidzeh!*"

The Garthim-Master gaped in consternation. As Emperor, his orders had not been carried out. As Garthim-Master, his professional vanity had been blistered.

"*Howtee oo mee Kelffinks,*" he said finally, in a voice slow with bewilderment.

"Of course I'm no Gelfling," Aughra snapped back at him. "*Katakontidzeh tekka!*" She wheeled on the Garthim and cursed them as well, although she knew it was an empty gesture. She glowered at the Skeksis again. Since her emergence from the sack, all but two had neglected their feast: the Gourmand, and the Ritual-Master, who now felt he could stomach a few choice tidbits torn from the Nebrie's breast. "I'll get my eye to you all," Aughra swore. "I'll settle your aspects semisquare and *quincunx.*"

To assuage his humiliation, the Garthim-Master also flung oaths and threats at the Garthim. Such an outburst was pointless, everyone knew that. The Garthim were terrible but ignorant tools of the Garthim-Master. They did what they were told to do. They acted without question. They made no excuses. They had been sent to Aughra's house, and they had brought back what they captured. All the Garthim-Master had achieved by his tantrum was to make himself look foolish.

The Ritual-Master now took charge of the situation. With a calmness calculated to shame the Garthim-Master's ire, he stepped over to Aughra, who shrank from his flaccid flesh. "*Svaleros ho Kelffinks,*" he stated.

Aughra cackled with cold mirth. She already knew the Gelfling was dangerous to the Skeksis. She knew the prophecy; indeed, she had cast the charts and shuffled the cards that confirmed it.

Still calm, the Ritual-Master pointed out the obvious, that the Gelfling had to be killed. "*Kataftheeressthou.*" Therefore, he asked Aughra to tell him where it was. "*Poostitoc?*"

"Gone!" Aughra screamed at the Ritual-Master, and in her rage she threw back her head and laughed hollowly. "Gone! Gelfling gone. Was in my home, Gelfling. Not hard to catch him there, if you clever. But what you do? You burn my house." She sneered. "Gelfling gone. *Porroh klet!* Burn! Ruin! Conflagration! Orrery destroyed. No more orrery, now how you make predictions, huh? And why? Because you send Garthim. Stupid Garthim! Stupid, stupid, stupid! *Katakontidzeh!*"

She paused, wondering whether to compound the Skeksis' confusion by confiding that the runaway Gelfling had found the true shard. She was in a state to do almost anything to spite them at this moment. But the inveterate habit of not telling everything she knew, the trademark of the seer, gave her pause. Besides, that was a vital piece of intelligence.

While she was pondering, the Garthim-Master reasserted his authority by barking out commands. With one eye on the Ritual-Master, he ordered the Scientist and the Slave-Master to take Aughra to the Chamber of Life. "*Aukhra na Rakhash!*" Without her orrery, she was not of much use to the Skeksis. He shouted another order to the Garthim, to return to their pit. "*Garthim na bullorkhskaunga!*" Then he sat down at the table again and resumed tearing at the Nebrie's roasted flesh, to show that he had nothing to worry about.

As Aughra was dragged away, she could not resist a few enigmatic taunts. "*Kakofrontez!*" she snarled. "Now prophecy is. Prophecy of Gelfling. Gelfling come get you, Skeksis fools. You see. And Aughra know when. Aughra know when is what and what shall be when. Oh yes. Oh yes."

The Ritual-Master had been waiting to play his trump card. The one essential step that must now be taken had been overlooked by the Garthim-Master. The Ritual-Master would take it instead, and no one could accuse him of presumption at such a critical juncture.

He threw back his head and called up into the vaulted ceiling, "*Kelffinks makhun kim.*"

Crowded together on ledges overlooking the banquet hall were the Crystal Bats, each grasping its spy crystal. At the Ritual-Master's order, they awakened, and from the flock there arose a chill, shrilling sound. One by one they spread their wings and took off flying out into the purple twilight through a high, open window. Usually their mission was simply to reconnoiter the whole landscape, transmitting back to the castle information that would give the Skeksis a broad surveillance of their tyrannized world; but this time they had received from the Ritual-Master a specific command: Find the Gelfling.

From the castle tower, they launched out in all directions, on their slowly beating wings.

Bone/nail

fading into
flesh, wrinkle
scales sin
etc

membane

↖ THUMB
UNDERNEA

SIZE

wrinkles
or knobs

Brian Froud

CHAPTER IV
IN COUNTRY MIRTH

Kira led Jen through the swamplands to the bank of a river. It was a broad river, flowing lazily, but what was most striking about it was that its water was as black as a crow's wing. It gleamed and rippled murmurously in the setting suns, whose reflected beams blazed from it like polished copper. Jen knelt on the bank and cupped water in his hands to see whether the river was simply gorged on dark mud from the swamp. No, the water was black. It ran through his fingers, leaving no sediment.

He looked over his shoulder at Kira, standing behind him, and confessed to her his fear of the color black.

She nodded. "I know. I used to have that fear, too. The Garthim, wasn't it?"

"I suppose so," Jen said. "I never knew why."

"And now you've seen them again and escaped from them."

Jen smiled ruefully. "So now, you think, I ought to be able to conquer my fear."

"I conquered mine." In Kira's voice was the hint of a challenge. Then she knelt beside him and put her arm around his neck. "It was because of this river that I learned to conquer it. I love this river. You'll see why. Come on." And she led him along the bank.

She was right, of course, Jen reflected. He could not spend the rest of his life in fear of a color. There was no shame in fearing a thing like the Garthim. Only a fool would be reckless with them, a short-lived fool. But black was the color of the sky between stars, the color of a burnt stick, of crows, or his eyelids when he slept, and no tyranny of darkness could enlist everything black. She said she loved this river and he would see why. Jen trusted Kira. In dreamfasting he had told her of his time by the waterfalls pining for the company of another Gelfling. She, too, had been lonely. Now they had to trust each other, or else the world, transformed by their chance meeting, would become a place without meaning or future after all, a place merely of chance.

Hauled up on the riverbank was a shell, the husk of a dead beetle. Kira pushed it down onto the water, and Fizzgig leaped into the boat, obviously at home in it. Kira followed. "Come on," she said again.

Jen climbed in, and Kira with a pole ready in the boat, pushed them off.

They floated away, on the black river, gently rocking as they drifted with the current. They left the swamplands and came into a stretch where the river ran between low cliffs, on top of which trees arched over on both sides. Kira was reclining with one hand trailing in the water. Jen, too, relaxed, lullabied by the motion of the boat.

He became aware of a sound all around them. It was like a humming chorus, quiet enough for him to have missed it until he relaxed. He looked at the banks of the river to see what was causing it.

Kira noticed and smiled. "This is something you haven't heard before," she said.

"No, I haven't. What is it? Where's it coming from?"

She did not answer. Instead, she began to sing, and what she sang had no words. She opened her throat and chanted a long melodic line in one breath, all with her lips slightly apart. It was a melody in the Lydian mode, and to Jen it sounded ancient, although he did not recognize it from the tunes the urRu had taught him. In the union of her voice and the melody was sorrow and its transfiguration into acceptance and wonder. Jen hardly dared to breathe at such beauty. Then he ached to respond. When her breath-line had expired and she prepared for another, he lifted his flute and this time played a simple counterpoint to her song. Even as he played, he could hear the sounds around them, which were in perfect harmony. Fizzgig stopped fidgeting and gazed over the side of the boat at his reflection in the glossy black water.

"Do you know now?" Kira asked. "Do you know where those sounds are coming from?"

Jen gestured helplessly. "I... it seems to be everywhere, in the trees and the river, and... no, I don't know."

"That's it," Kira laughed. "Look, that moss there, it hums. Listen to it." Jen listened and heard. "Now the trees," Kira told him. "It's something like a whistle, or a sigh. And you see the bubbles on the water. Listen to them, Jen. You must always listen. There is always music to be heard. You can hear the percussion of the water rippling. The music we make is only a part of it. Now do you see why I love this river?"

As an answer, Jen raised his flute and started to play again, as attentive as he could be to the chorus he was joining. Kira waiting awhile, then added her voice, lower this time, harmonizing.

The boat slowly turned, in the arms of the river, as the current bore them along in the twilight, and they made their music with the music that would have been there even without them.

Jen thought of all that urSol the Chanter had taught him about technique, and he was very glad to have that skill, since it enabled him to make a better, more considered contribution; but urSol had never taught him this, that music is revealed, not invented. From the banks he could now hear yet more threads in the tapestry of sound: a tiny ringing as of bells, a deeper gonglike note, and the cries of birds. Nothing was discordant.

Low on the horizon, the suns spread a lace of rose-colored light over the surface of the black river. Kira sang her melody. Always it seemed to be the same one, yet she had such command of inflections and subtly varied intervals that each breath-line disclosed a new modulation. Jen continued to harmonize. He thought he could find no better way to spend the rest of his life than this. If the boat had slowly sunk beneath the water, he felt he would not have minded.

Abruptly, Fizzgig started to bark. Kira, at the same time, glanced upward, pushed Jen down flat in the boat, then ducked her head, and lay curled up.

"What is it?" Jen asked urgently.

She answered in a whisper, "Up there. A Crystal Bat. Don't move."

"A what?"

"I'll explain later."

"A spy crystal? Someone I met mentioned them."

"Same thing. The Pod People call them Crystal Bats."

"How do you know what it is?" Jen asked.

"I saw a flash of light from the crystal in its claws."

Kira had been quietly taking something from the pouch on her belt. Then she stood up. Around her head she was swinging a double-weighted thong. When she let go, it whizzed into the air directly above their heads. There was a squeaking, flapping noise, then a splash. More splashing. Then silence.

Kira said, "I hit it." She was not boasting, just stating a fact.

Jen was awed. "Are there many of those?"

"More and more all the time," she answered. "What they see, with their crystals, the Skeksis see, too."

"How did you learn to do that, the way you brought it down?"

"The Pod People in my village taught me. They've had to learn it for their own protection. Otherwise, they'd be in slavery by now. In many other Pod villages, all the people have been taken. The Crystal Bats are the only creatures they will kill. Except the Skeksis and their Garthim, of course. But they have no chance against them."

"How do you know the spy crystal hadn't already seen us?"

"I don't know. But I don't think it did. It would have hovered near us if it had. It didn't seem to be hovering, did it?" Kira sighed. "What I ought to do is make sure it's dead. I would if it were daylight. All we can do is hope."

As they floated on, Jen told Kira about the crystal shard, and the torn and tattered words of bidding that urSu, and then urZah, had given him, and what had happened at Aughra's house. He brought the shard out from his tunic to show her. It gleamed in the twilight. "I know that what I have to do is… it's something to do with the Skeksis. I don't know what, though. And I don't know who will tell me."

Behind them, upriver, the Crystal Bat had dragged itself out of the mud, shaken off the thong, and was now cautiously gliding just above the surface of the black stream, on their track.

Far away from the river, the urRu had closed up their caves. The time had come, at last, to leave the valley. In a long, plodding procession headed by urZah, one following another in their dusty garments, leaning on their sticks, they ascended the spiral path and started to cross the plain.

Fizzgig was the first to sense that the boat was nearing the village. He became restless and started to make a little whining noise. Jen stared downstream. Soon he could see lights and hear the sound of busy voices. Then Kira used the pole to maneuver the beetle shell into the bank. Fizzgig jumped out and the two Gelfling followed, beaching the boat.

It was too dark for them to see that the Crystal Bat was hovering just a little way upriver, reflecting in its spy crystal every step they took.

They were making their way through the underbrush of the wilderness when two Pod People jumped up in front of them, holding out long staffs in a challenging gesture.

"It's all right," Kira cried out quickly in Pod speech. "It's me, Kira. I have a friend with me."

At once the Pod guards lowered their staffs and joyfully ran up to greet Kira. Jen clearly puzzled them but they were willing to take Kira's word that he was a friend.

Preceded by the guards, Jen and Kira emerged from the bushes into a clearing. In the center of it were several long houses. The convex outer shell of each house was formed from the seed pod of some gigantic plant, split down the middle and laid flat to the ground, thus raising a striated dome. Doorways, windows, and chimneys had been neatly carved out and framed in wood. Through these apertures a cheerful firelight shone from each house. Everywhere, people could be seen bustling around, within and between their houses.

Notwithstanding the disguise of dusk, Jen recognized the place from Kira's description of it in dreamfasting. It was her home, and these were Pod People. As she took his hand to introduce him into the village, he knew that the largest of the long houses was the one where she dwelt.

Fizzgig bounced on ahead of them, barking enthusiastically. The peasants looked up, peering into the dusk. When they saw Kira, they ran up to greet her, whooping with delight in their babbling, lilting speech. Then they stopped short, hesitating, crowding together in confusion.

"They can't believe their eyes," Kira said, "seeing you."

"Will they welcome me?" Jen asked.

"Oh, *yes*. When they see that I am happy with you."

From the largest house an old woman came running out past the others, who were still hesitating. She threw out her arms and embraced Kira.

Again, Jen knew at once who it was: Ydra, Kira's foster mother. But he felt he ought to wait to be introduced, nevertheless. It was going to raise a few ticklish questions, this dreamfasting.

Ydra greeted Jen with a warm smile when Kira introduced them, but the old woman was clearly as confused to see two Gelfling as they themselves had been on meeting each other in the swamp. After Aughra, then Kira, and now, Ydra, it was obvious to Jen that the whole world had hitherto assumed that only one Gelfling still lived on Thra. If there were two, might there not be still more in some other corner of the planet? It was thrilling to think so.

At the doorway of the largest house, the Pod People surrounded the Gelfling. Jen was solemnly welcomed over the threshold. Leaf, twig, root, and fruit were extended for him to hold. Then, at Kira's bidding, he was required to drop each one to the ground, where the pattern they made with each other on falling was examined for auguries. Since everyone went on being jolly, Jen hoped that the prospects looked encouraging. One step over the threshold, he was again bidden to pause while he chewed and swallowed a seed they gave him, and drank from a gourd—kainz juice, he recognized. The Pod People laughed at how thirstily he drank from their loving cup. The truth was he was famished again.

He saw that he would not have long to wait. In the single room under the Pod roof, kettles of soup were steaming as cooks stirred them, and a long table was already laid with platters of cheese and vegetables, katyaken-egg flans, gourd mush, dyillorkin seeds, river roots and berries, loaves of bellow-bread, and bowls of juice and milk. The Pod People seemed to be continually singing as they prepared their feast. Jen wondered whether his visit luckily coincided with a festival supper. No, Kira told him, it was like this every night in the Pod village. Why should it be otherwise? The simple, natural foods were in abundant supply, and song was not subject to drought.

In addition to the happiness of the place, the aroma of good food, and his joy in Kira's company, Jen felt very good about one other fact: he was a full head taller than any of the Pod People. That was a brand-new experience for him, after a childhood among the urRu. He really felt himself almost a giant when he looked into the cribs of the smallest Podling infants.

Ydra wanted Jen to follow her. She led him to the head of the table, where two chairs with arms had been set, side by side. Ydra motioned to him to sit down. Jen looked at Kira. "Go on," Kira said. "You are the guest of honor tonight."

"Sit down with me at the same time," Jen asked.

"All right."

Grinning, they took their seats. The Pod People joined them, sitting on stools that had been placed along each side of the long table. A small band struck up a merry tune on reed pipes and gourd drums. Loud chattering and laughter filled the house as the cooks served the soup. Jen looked at Kira and thought he had never been so happy in all his life. She did not need to take his hand to acknowledge that she felt the same way.

Hoping not to betray quite how ravenous he was, Jen started to eat. The Pod People had been waiting for the opportunity to learn about their visitor. With Kira's help as translator, and picking up a few words of Pod speech as he went along, Jen managed to tell them a little about himself. It seemed they had never heard of the urRu. When Jen first described them, the Pod People began to seem fearful of him. "*Shkekshe?*" one of them asked. Jen shook his head firmly. Kira explained to them that the urRu were indeed as huge as the Skeksis but a peaceful race. The Pod People nodded, partly reassured.

He brought out the shard to show to the Pod People. Though they found it pretty, it too held no meaning for them. Jen was disappointed. He had hoped that they might give him a clue to the mission he was supposed to accomplish with it.

Between conversations with the peasants, and the eating and drinking, he took in the interior of the house. It had been furnished with absolute simplicity. Nothing was decorative; everything served a purpose. The furniture was solid. What beauty it had was the beauty of both usefulness and usage. The chairs, the tables, the platters and spoons, all were made of wood, and shone with the rich patina of age and handling.

As the evening wore on, the music grew faster and noisier, and some of the peasants started to dance to it. Jen was fascinated. He had never seen anything like this. The dancers began by energetically bouncing about on their own. Then they linked hands in groups of four or five and leaped around in circles. Gradually the circles were linked to each other, and eventually all the dancers were holding hands in one great, bounding ring. When the music reached a climax, the ring broke at one point and the line of dancers coiled themselves inward to form a tightening spiral. At the finish they were all packed close against each other, jigging up and down so enthusiastically that the old house shook.

"What's it all for?" Jen asked.

"Dancing?" Kira replied.

"Yes."

"What a funny question. I don't think it's *for* anything. It's just fun."

Jen nodded, no wiser.

"You know how to dance, don't you, Jen?" Kira asked. "You just sing with your body."

"I don't know." He shook his head. "The urRu didn't teach me about dancing."

After a brief pause for refreshment, amid much laughter, the band struck up again, more wildly than ever.

From her pouch, Kira brought out a length of string and made a simple cat's cradle on her fingers. Then she transferred it to Jen's, pulled out more loops, took it back, and transferred it again, all the time making it more complicated. With beaming faces, the Pod People watched them. Fizzgig had fallen asleep at Kira's feet.

Jen looked at Kira as she frowned thoughtfully at the cat's cradle. "How long may we stay here?" he asked.

"As long as we want," she answered, pulling out two more loops.

"Then I don't ever want to leave."

She paused and looked up at him. "What about the crystal shard?"

Jen closed his eyes. "Whatever it is that I am supposed to do with the shard, it cannot make me as perfectly happy as I am here. With you."

One of the peasants, grinning, leaned over and asked Jen *Lyepa Kira?* Others around heard him and giggled.

"What did he say?" Jen asked.

Kira smiled but would not tell him.

Fizzgig had woken up. His face was alert, listening. He gave a little growl.

Kira looked down at him fondly and scratched him between the ears. "I don't think Fizzgig approves of you now," she smiled. Then her expression became more serious. "Jen, it was only because of your quest that you and I met each other. That in itself should give you the courage to go on with it."

Fizzgig growled again, more loudly.

Jen was thinking about Kira's remark when the band struck up again, with more vigor and noise than ever. Ydra came up to the table and invited Jen to dance with her.

"Go on," Kira bade him. "You can do more eating afterward."

Jen grinned sheepishly. "Is it so obvious how hungry I am?"

He stood up. Ydra took his hand and led him to an area of the room where several Pod People had already started to dance again. Everybody clapped when they saw Jen take the floor.

Guided by Ydra, he found he had no trouble at all in stepping and skipping to the changing rhythms, up and down, round and round. Those Pod People who were not dancing crowded in to watch, cheering, beating time, and tossing seeds and fragrant petals. Ydra began to sing a wordless song, a lively version of the one Kira had sung in the boat on the black river. Jen, in turn, played his flute, along with the raucous band.

Soon the whole room was dancing. Only Kira, Jen saw, was still at the table. The cat's cradle was on her fingers, but she was not attending to it. She had her head cocked in the air as though she were straining to hear a sound from outside the uproarious room.

In vivacious celebration of their happiness, the Pod People were shouting and clapping and stamping their feet to a climax. The din was such that nobody heard Fizzgig barking very loudly.

And then a hideous noise of cracking lacerated the room as one side of the shell house was smashed in. Splinters flew among the crowded dancers.

A great hole had been torn in the wall, and through it came a huge black claw.

It withdrew for a moment, then gashed a larger breach. A Garthim battered its way in. Others trampled through after it.

In the panic stampede, the Pod People skittered in all directions, crashing into furniture, howling with terror. Some escaped through the door or out the windows. Some were seized in Garthim claws and crushed to death instantly. Others were picked up by their heads or arms or feet and stuffed into round wicker cages that the Garthim carried on their backs. In the chaotic din of destruction and death, Jen ran desperately toward the table where he had been sitting with Kira. It had been overturned onto its side and Kira was crouched behind it, with Fizzgig. On the floor beside her lay her cat's cradle, a mere tangled bunch of string.

Jen crouched down with her. "It's us they're after," he gasped.

Kira nodded. "That Crystal Bat, on the river."

Jen peered out over the top edge of the table. The scattered cooking fires had set the ruined house alight, but through the thickening smoke Jen saw one of the Garthim almost upon them, hurling aside everything in its path. Jen stood up in front of Kira, protectively. From his tunic he snatched the shard, the only thing he had that at all resembled a weapon. He gripped it like a dagger.

The Garthim towered over him now, its great serrated claw descending and grabbing his arm. With his free hand, Jen stabbed wildly at the black thing. As the shard struck the Garthim's claw, it rang out with a deep, resonant note. The note resounded around the globe of Thra. Far out, on the plain, the urRu heard it. They paused in their trek and raised their old heads, listening.

The Garthim released its hold on Jen and drew back from him, into the dense smoke. Behind it, however, other Garthim pressed forward toward the upturned table. All of them had located their quarry when they heard the note of the shard. Repel them as he might, Jen knew that they were so huge that each assault they made was going to wound him badly before he could strike back. It was only a matter of time before he was killed, and then Kira. His wounded arm was already useless. It dangled from his shoulder. Blood was staining his tunic.

On the hand with which he gripped the shard, he felt the touch of another hand: Kira's. It told him the way to the door through the blinding smoke, it told him of the forest outside, it told of freedom.

Hand in hand they ran, still crouching to avoid the thickest fumes. Fizzgig did not leave Kira's heels. They passed within inches of Garthim, who, though invulnerable to flames, were now shown to be as blinded by smoke as any sighted creature. On their massive, plated feet, they were staggering in confusion toward the upturned table, randomly destroying whatever they collided with. The floor was a mess of Pod blood and flesh, splinters, food scraps, smashed pots.

As the Gelfling neared the door, a Garthim loomed up through the clouds in front of them. They froze. They could see only the lower half of its body. It lumbered away from them, itself seeking the clear air outside, smashing a path for itself through the walls. Jen and Kira waited to see which way it would turn, then bolted out of the house behind the Garthim's back.

The scene they beheld outside was a desolate one. Smoke poured from every house in the village. All of them had been torn apart by the Garthim in their insensate hunt for the Gelfling. The cries of Pod People who had been collected as casual booty wailed on the night air.

Jen and Kira had no time to stand and stare in pity. They sprinted into the low brush at the margin of the forest. But they were not quick enough. One of the Garthim had spotted them. They heard it behind them, clattering and pounding in pursuit, closing in on them rapidly. As they ran, they both knew it was hopeless. At every stride they expected a claw to seize one of them from behind, crushing their bones and flesh to a pulp. Jen grasped the shard tightly. He would fight to his last breath.

Then, from the line of trees where the forest began, a thing yet more terrifying than the Garthim emerged, watching them with cold reptilian eyes. Kira screamed, and Fizzgig set up a frenzy of barking at the monster that had appeared in front of them.

It was the Chamberlain, still decked in motley rags. His taloned hand was raised in a gesture of arrest.

Still running, Jen and Kira took the only escape left to them, veering off through the brush parallel to the forest margin.

The Garthim, however, two strides behind them, halted at the Chamberlain's gesture. The Skeksis repeated it, and the Garthim, hesitantly, turned round and lumbered back toward the raped village.

When they realized that the noise of pursuit had stopped, Jen and Kira stumbled to a halt, panting. Turning to look behind them, they saw, bewildered, the Garthim making its way back to the rest of the troop. They saw Kira's home, smoke billowing from the gashes in its side, and other houses wrecked, and the vast shadows of the Garthim gathering the hysterical Pod People in their claws. And they saw the thing a distance away in the brush, its head turned on its long neck, watching them. It made another gesture to them. But it was not moving in pursuit of them.

Exhausted, they walked into the forest. As they began to push their way through the undergrowth, bracken and shrub and fern, pathetic sounds from the village they had abandoned still rang in their ears.

Kira was weeping. "That was my home," she sobbed. "I grew up among those people. In that house. And now, it... I saw Ydra. They picked her up by her hair and tossed her into a sack. Like a cabbage. An old woman. The Garthim... Oh, Jen..."

Jen said nothing. He put his unwounded arm tightly around

her shoulders for what comfort he could offer, but he could think of nothing to say. Because of his quest he had met Kira. That was what she had said. And because of his quest her people had been massacred. That she did not have to say.

Brian Froud

CHAPTER V
AT THE HOUSES OF
THE OLD ONES

Kira was at home in the forest. Having often played there as a child, she knew the paths and the glades. Follow her, she told Jen, and she would find her way, even in the dark night, to a soft bank she knew in a secluded, safe place where they could sleep in comfort. It was not far, she said. Both of them, exhausted, ravaged by visions of horror, needed to sleep. And Jen's arm, although it had stopped bleeding, ached with every step he took. Kira said she could heal it with a moss the Pod People used. She would find some in the forest.

Jen was preoccupied with what he had witnessed. He felt himself tremble and was grateful for Kira's company. Although the night had been even more harrowing for her, she was the one who had found the courage to be calm, to do what had to be done.

Brambles scratched their skin as they pushed deeper into the forest. Any creature could be lurking in the darkness under the trees. "Not far now," Kira said encouragingly. Jen tried hard to ignore the throbbing in his arm. Never before had he known so much agony. Each time his right foot landed on the ground, a stabbing pain shot through that side of his body. When they reached the bank that Kira had remembered, Jen sank down with a groan of relief. He had almost fallen asleep before Kira found the healing moss and took the shard to cut strips of moss from the ground. Then she bound them around his arm.

"Are we safe here, do you think?" Jen asked groggily.

Kira was concentrating on his arm. "Well," she finally said, "I think there are too many trees over us for the Crystal Bats to find us."

Against the pale moonlight of the sky, Jen could see that she was right. Although they were in a glade of sorts, the high branches of the trees met above them, like fingertips touching. Behind them, as they sat on the bank, was the thick undergrowth through which they had forced their way. Facing them, across the glade, was a dark horizontal cutting off the paler sky, the edge of a low cliff, perhaps. It certainly felt like a secluded and sheltered spot. But it was not the Crystal Bats that he most feared now, nor even the Garthim, of which they were harbingers. No, what luridly preyed on his mind was the horrible apparition that had slouched out from the forest and confronted them as they were fleeing.

He had known at once what it was, by instinct he supposed. To confirm his suspicions, he asked Kira, "That monster that tried to stop us—that was a Skeksis, wasn't it?"

Kira tenderly wound the last bandage of moss around his arm and fastened it with a knotted stalk. "Yes," she said quietly, "I'm sure it was. I've not seen one since the day my mother was killed by one, when I was still a baby, but it had talons like those I remember. And some of the Pod People have shown me Skeksis in dreamfasting. Yes."

Jen sighed and lay on his back, watching the clouds feather the sky between the branches. His feelings about the Skeksis were ambiguous. In a way, it was almost a relief. If he had beheld a thing so ghastly and then been told that it was not a Skeksis, that he had yet to experience facing a Skeksis, he would have felt the world outside the valley of the urRu to be too desperate a place for him to live. And yet, if he persevered in his quest, there was every indication that eventually he would be required to confront the Skeksis, in some way to oppose a number—how many?–of creatures as fearsome as the one he had just seen. What possible chance could a Gelfling have against opponents so vicious in appearance, so huge? But then he recognized a further ambiguity in his feelings—about the giant bulk of that Skeksis there had been something vaguely familiar to one who had been raised among the urRu.

"Do you think it will be coming after us?" Jen asked.

"It didn't look as though it would, did it?" Kira replied. "The Pod People say the Skeksis always use the Garthim for their hunting because they aren't terribly good at it themselves. No, I think they'll send their Crystal Bats out again."

"Then we must stay here in the forest," Jen said, "and always keep under cover of the trees."

"What, forever?" Kira asked.

"If necessary," Jen said. He looked at her. "Would you mind that?"

"Sooner or later they'd find us, somehow." Kira shrugged. "In any case, what about this?"

She handed the shard back to Jen. He took it and looked at it wearily. "Yes," he said, "*what* about this? It has already been responsible for the mutilation of your village. I hate it."

He sat up and hurled the shard from him as far as he could. They heard it fall among the leaves on the other side of the glade. Fizzgig thought of fetching it but decided against it, on account of the darkness.

"Things can't be responsible for anything," Kira observed. "Only those who use them can be."

Jen felt ashamed of himself. He said nothing.

Kira sat down beside him on the bank. "Jen," she said, "I know what you're feeling. But it's not your *fault* it happened."

"It wouldn't have happened but for me."

"That's not the same thing. You could just as well say it wouldn't have happened but for me either. If I hadn't seen you in the swamp, or if I'd just run away from you—and I nearly did, in fact—then the village wouldn't have been destroyed. Well, not tonight, anyway. But in the end, the Skeksis and the Garthim will continue to rule as they always have done, and any village might be discovered and destroyed at any time. They come and capture the Pod People in order to use them as slaves, you know."

"What about the Gelfling? Did they destroy all of our people?"

"That's what I was always told—except for me. The Pod People kept me hidden, and then taught me how to hide myself. And now here you are."

"So why do you think that Skeksis sent the Garthim away when it could have killed us within a few steps?"

"I have no idea."

"It was almost as though the Skeksis wanted to save us."

Kira laughed without mirth. "I can't believe that. The Skeksis have never cared for anything but themselves, that's what the Pod People always say."

"But suppose they say that because they have always been tyrannized by the Skeksis. Suppose the Skeksis have more feelings for the Gelfling."

"I saw one of them kill my mother."

"Yes," Jen said miserably. "And there's no doubt who those Garthim were really after."

"No, there isn't."

Jen shut his eyes with the despair of it all. Soon, his body took pity on his mind and let sleep watch over him. Kira lay down on the bank beside him and also slept. The moon moved its shadows silently across their faces.

Jen awoke to daylight and to Kira's face smiling down at him. His head was in her lap.

"Where are we?" Jen asked.

"We are safe," Kira replied.

"What a wonderful thing to hear the moment you awake!" Jen smiled back at her and sat up. He winced, feeling his arm.

"How is it?" Kira asked.

Jen moved it backward and forward, carefully. "Better," he announced. "A lot better, I think. A bit stiff, though."

"Leave the moss on for now, all the same."

Jen inspected his green arm and grinned at the sight. Then he stood up and glanced around the glade. Fizzgig stood up with him and began to romp among the flowers.

"Did you sleep?" Jen asked.

"Of course I did."

"With my head in your lap?"

"You were groaning a bit but it didn't stop me falling back to sleep. On the contrary."

"What's that?" Jen was staring across the glade. What he had taken, in the darkness, to be the edge of a low cliff he now saw to be the façade of a ruined building.

"It's the house of the Old Ones."

"The Old Ones?" Jen repeated, intensely curious. A strange sense of intimacy with the house at once took possession of him. "Who are they?"

Kira shrugged. "I don't know. That's what the Pod People always call them, the Old Ones." She seemed reluctant to say any more.

"Have you ever seen them, the Old Ones?"

"No. I don't think anyone lives there now."

Jen was wandering toward a dilapidated doorway. He was enchanted by the ruins, which he now saw were more than just the one house. Through the doorway, other walls and courtyards came into view. The stonework was graceful, with the remains of carvings evident here and there. The floors, where they were not covered with debris from the caved-in roofs, were apparently tiled.

"Don't go in, Jen." Kira's voice was suddenly tense.

"Why not?"

"I was told not to. Ever."

"Why? What's the danger?"

"I don't know. The roofs might fall in on you. The Pod People would never go inside. Bad things happened here once. The Old Ones were killed by the Skeksis. Jen?"

"I have to." Jen meant exactly what he said. No mere idle curiosity was luring him into the ruins but an affinity he immediately felt with the place. He could not begin to explain it. He was being drawn inside, that was all he knew.

As if to confirm his impulse, lying in the doorway among the leaves was the shard, the blade of its dagger shape pointing inside the ruins like a compass needle. Jen hesitated a moment, then decided not to retrieve it. That was a decision he would rather defer for now. He walked through the doorway.

Then he turned round, looking back at Kira. "Come on," he said and held out his hand.

She gazed at him, doubtful and anxious.

More persuasively he repeated, "Come on, Kira. We must see what's in here."

With a slow shrug and pursing her lips, she crossed the glade. At the doorway she stopped. "I'm afraid," she muttered to herself, almost in apology.

Jen did not hear her. He had already turned back and was stepping cautiously into the ruined building.

Kira, too, noticed the shard lying on the ground. She picked it up and placed it in her pouch. Then, scooping up Fizzgig and clutching him close to her, she followed Jen into the ruins.

Everything Jen saw delighted him, in its proportions and workmanship, in its deft taste in decoration. Though ruined, the buildings still possessed a dignity, a noble bearing. He walked along a passage, then another at right angles. Doorways opened onto small chambers that no longer bore any trace of their furnishings. The roofs, it seemed, had been thatched, or at least covered in some kind of vegetable matter, branches perhaps, to judge by the litter of dead wood and shriveled fronds on the floor. Where any roofing at all remained, it consisted only of a few joists, now open to the sky. Throughout, the floors were tiled in terra-cotta. On some of the tiles traces of a pattern could be seen, but never in sufficient number to convey the meaning of the grand design. Windows had been plentiful. In many places now, the wall had collapsed above the lintel, leaving a sort of crenellation. Bushes and grasses had taken up habitation, as had scuttling spiders.

Around the next corner, an open archway led into a much larger and lighter room than Jen had previously seen. On the walls were scraps of fabric, faded and tattered evidence of some richer hangings, tapestries possibly. Most striking of all, in the middle of a long wall stood a chair of curious and elliptical design. In size, it would have suited Jen handsomely. He was trying to clear it of leaf mold, fungi, and cobwebs when Kira joined him.

What he discovered, as he brushed and scraped away the debris of time, was not so much a chair as a throne. It seemed to be fashioned from a single piece of material, marble perhaps. The light struck iridescent gleams from it. No, it was not marble but some more delicate material, which softly glistened like mother-of-pearl. Was the throne hewn from the shell of one giant mollusc? It seemed to be so, for no joints were apparent. What could now be seen, fetching gasps of admiration from both Gelfling, was that the throne had been intricately inlaid with filigree designs in bright metal and gems. Kira started helping Jen clean the throne, while Fizzgig interestedly sniffed around the corners of the large room.

Finally it stood revealed—chair, throne, seat, whatever it was—a thing so intimately responsive to the light that at the slightest movement of their heads they would see it shimmer through a thousand transmuted rainbows. Kira kept her head as still as she could, yet the iridian glitter continued to change as though answering the atomically measured dance of the suns.

While Jen looked around to see what other wonders he might discover, Kira, spellbound, approached the chair and, with reverence, seated herself on it. Its back reached exactly up to the height of her head, and her hands lay comfortably on the arms of the chair. "It might have been made for me," she pronounced.

Jen glanced back at her and gave her a respectful bow. "You look like a queen in it," he said.

Kira nodded, smiling. She would not have confessed it to him, but the truth was that she felt like a queen. She closed her eyes. It was at once easier to imagine those who dwelt here in their glory than not to imagine them. She could almost hear them—their voices, their music—and feel their touch. The Pod People, deeply superstitious about this place, believing it haunted by spirits, had not told her who its former inhabitants, "the Old Ones," had been. Now, with a shiver of intuition, she knew for herself.

Jen had moved on through a grand archway at the farthest end of the room, where a magnificently carved wooden door studded with iron stood ajar. He was now standing in a long room, a gallery of sorts. The roof had collapsed, as had all the others, but the walls had remained nearly intact. And what he saw on one of the walls caused him to cry out. "Kira! Come quickly!"

"I know," Kira said to herself, leaving the throne to join Jen, "I know. They were Gelfling."

The plastered wall Jen was gazing at was covered with frescoes or, rather, one long fresco, framed within a broad, elaborately detailed border. Many creatures and events were pictured, but there was no doubt who the protagonists were. Gelfling, in costumes of antique nobility, formed the centerpiece of each tableau. Apart from their robes, the figures could have been those of Jen and Kira. For both of them, it was like coming home at last. In awe, they stared at what they knew must be their ancestors, the lost-and-found story of themselves: a Gelfling queen enthroned, attended by an aged vizier and young courtiers bearing flowers, and around them Gelfling farmers, carpenters, smiths crafting jewelry, dancers, celebrants with pokals, and musicians, including a long-haired Gelfling girl playing a forked flute that replicated Jen's. Between each tableau were emblems of trees or leaves.

As they gazed at the pictures, painted in earth colors, it became evident to them that not just a way of life was being celebrated here, but that a narrative was being unfolded. In the broad border, which ran around the entire perimeter of the fresco, they began to recognize images. A Gelfling village was destroyed by Garthim. Above a mountain, three concentric suns were depicted within a triangle—the Great Conjunction, Jen assumed, judging from Aughra's demonstration. Depicted next was a Crystal emitting a beam of light, and encircling the Crystal were eighteen creatures—Jen counted them—which might have been Skeksis or even, he thought, the urRu. The Crystal was pictured again, but this time it was darker in color and an even darker dagger-shaped form had been painted in it. Alongside this was a picture of the shard. "Look," Jen said astounded. "It's my crystal shard!" He felt for it, to compare it to the picture. It was gone. Then he remembered having thrown it away.

Kira smiled at him and, taking the shard from her pouch, held it up to the fresco. Shard and image were a perfect match.

Jen and Kira looked at each other, trying to unriddle the meaning. Kira offered the shard to Jen. He paused, then accepted it. He stared at the shard in his hand, then at the shard in the fresco, and back again. He looked at Kira. She was watching him closely.

Still holding her gaze, he returned the shard to his tunic. Memory of what urSu had once taught him returned: *Life presents more alternatives than choices.* Last night, Jen had seen his vision of evil. Here, in this room with Kira, he had found his vision of good. He was suffused with intention, the courage to act and to control the fear to which he had almost succumbed. He took Kira's hand and told her of his resolves. She nodded.

Their gaze returned to the riddles of the border. Next to the shard, two lines of creatures—eighteen in each line, Jen counted again—were pictured emerging from the Crystal, the lines radiating out in opposite directions. Unlike the earlier creatures, these were unambiguous. One line was of Skeksis, the other line of urRu. The mountain reappeared, this time transformed into the shape of a castle, at the center of which the Crystal was pictured once more. Kira and Jen then found themselves looking at the destruction of still more Gelfling by the Garthim, and the three concentric suns, and realized that their examination of the border had come full circle.

Now Kira pointed to a series of hieroglyphs that ran all the way around the outer edge of the border. "What are those?" she asked. "They're not pictures at all, are they?"

Jen looked closer. "No," he said. "They're runes."

"What are runes?"

"A kind of writing."

"Ah." Kira nodded. "Can you read them?"

"Yes."

"No one ever taught me to write or read," Kira said. "The Pod People have no need for it."

"I'll tell you what it says." Jen studied the hieroglyphs, wondering where the sentence began. Then he found a point at which the hieroglyphs were punctuated by a picture of the concentric suns surmounting the shard, and he read aloud starting from there:

> *When single shines the triple sun,*
> *What was sundered and undone*
> *Shall be whole, the two made one*
> *By Gelfling hand, or else by none.*

"Shall be whole," Jen repeated wonderingly. Make it whole, urSu had bidden him, heal the wound at the core of being. And urZah had added, reluctantly, make the dark light.

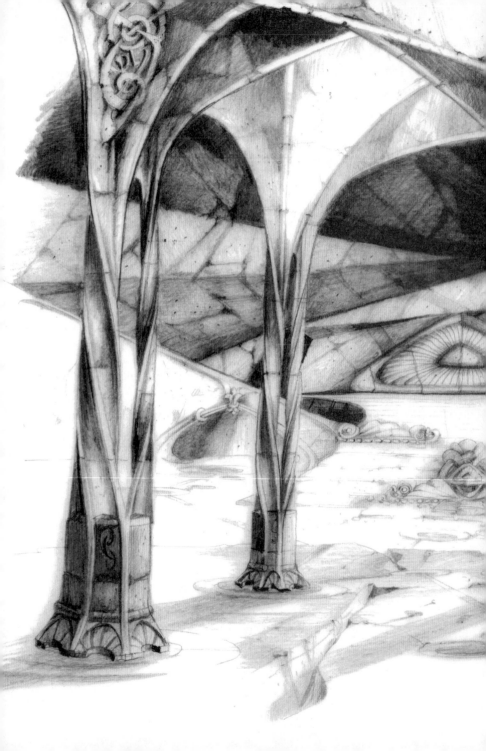

Jim Henson's Creature Shop

"Yes," Jen declared, his voice excited by comprehension at last. "I now know what I have to do." He looked at Kira and pointed to the frescoes. "Much of all this I still don't understand, but now it doesn't matter. I know what my part must be." He pulled out the shard again. "In the castle," he said, "there is a great Crystal. This shard was somehow broken from it. The consequence has been a wound in the world—evil. The Crystal has to be made whole again by a Gelfling. And I must restore this shard to the great Crystal in the castle." He paused. "And I will," he added quietly, placing the shard back inside his tunic. "I will."

Jen found himself laughing with relief—the relief of solving a riddle and of taking from it the energy needed to act on the solution. He looked at Kira. "Will you wait here for me?"

"Why, where are you going now?"

"To the castle. I have to be there at the time of the Great Conjunction of the sun brothers, 'when single shines the triple sun.' It will be very soon now. Aughra told me so."

"I'm coming, too," she said.

"No, Kira. I already have the destruction of your village on my conscience."

"And with no village now, where do you think I would go, on my own? Be brave, Jen. Accept what has happened and what must happen. Besides"–Kira smiled at him–"that prophecy you read there says '*by Gelfling hand.*' Is mine not a Gelfling hand?"

Before Jen could answer, Fizzgig looked up from sniffing in the corner of the room and started to growl. Kira was about to go and see what he had found when a shadow fell across all of them. They turned quickly.

The doorway was blocked by the gray bulk of a Skeksis, who was looking down at them. On the Chamberlain's face was an expression clearly intended to be ingratiating.

Fizzgig immediately bounded onto a windowsill and perched there, whimpering for Kira to follow him. She made as if to do so, in turn looking over her shoulder for Jen. He had not moved.

The Chamberlain raised his hand, talons sheathed, in a gesture resembling the one of the previous night. "Stay," he hissed. "Am friend. Friend to Kelffinks. Last night I save you from Garthim. Am I enemy? Am friend. Stay, please."

Jen looked up at the monster, which could have seized and crushed them in a trice. "I have been told that Skeksis kill Gelfling," he answered.

The Chamberlain snorted. "Pah. Is because stupid prophecy say Kelffinks end power of Skeksis. Stupid." He shook his head.

Jen was calculating that the Skeksis could not pass through the doorway unless he simply smashed down the walls, over which his head towered. But that did not seem to be the Skeksis' way, else why did they use the Garthim? No, with luck he and Kira could make a dash for it through the gaping hole of the window. Surreptitiously he edged back a few paces, to distance himself farther from the talons. Before escaping, however, he needed to find out all he could.

"Stupid prophecy," the monster was saying. "But Skeksis afraid. Fear Kelffinks, yes. Little Kelffinks! Mistake, much mistake. Stay, please. Am friend."

"Don't listen to it, Jen," Kira implored him. "It's a trick."

"What do you want with us?" Jen asked.

"Listen, please," the Chamberlain said. "Come with me, to castle. You will see, yes, I show to Skeksis you want peace, no? And not harm us. Please." The Chamberlain gestured again, this time beckoning Jen to approach.

Jen remained where he was. "Why should we trust you?" he asked. "You destroyed our race before. Look." He pointed to the frescoes.

The Chamberlain waved his hand dismissively. "Tired of killing. Tired of it. Of fear, too, yes. So am outcast from castle, you see?"

Jen nodded warily.

"But," the Chamberlain continued, "if bring peace back to castle, show Skeksis no fear of little Kelffinks, if do this, am not outcast then." He gestured again. "Come with me, please. Yes."

"If I come with you and make peace," Jen asked slowly, "will the Garthim attacks be stopped?"

The Chamberlain nodded vehemently.

"On the Pod People, too?"

"Yes. No more Garthim attacks. No more. Come, please, yes."

Jen hesitated, swayed by the pleading voice of the Skeksis. He looked round at Kira, who was still with Fizzgig by the window. She held out her hand to Jen, begging him to escape with her.

Jen looked back at the Skeksis. "I don't know," he said.

The Chamberlain smiled again, beseechingly. "Garthim energy come from Crystal in castle. Skeksis control Crystal. All power in Crystal. Soon"–the Chamberlain lifted his hands expressively–"soon much new power for Crystal."

"At the Great Conjunction?" Jen asked as casually as he could.

"Yes. You know of this?"

Jen shrugged and pointed vaguely to the frescoes again. "I have learned something of it from these pictures."

"Ah." The Chamberlain nodded. "Now, please come, yes. Please. Must be quick. Soon, much new power for Skeksis. Peace for Skeksis and Kelffinks hard then, much more hard after new power. Must be quick, now, please. Come?"

"Where to?"

"To castle. Show you way into castle with me, secret way, no

Garthim will see, through Teeth of Shkreesh, then we find Skeksis. Then we make peace, you and me together, and all good for Kelffinks. No more Garthim then. Come, please. Yes."

Kira ran forward to stand directly in front of Jen, her back to the Skeksis. She looked straight into Jen's eyes. "No, Jen," she said passionately. "Look." She pointed to the picture of the antique Gelfling civilization. "And look." Now her finger reminded him of the picture in which Garthim destroyed a Gelfling village. Her eyes searched his. "'*By Gelfling hand, or else by none,*'" she recited.

Jen reached out his hand to take Kira's. Together, they wheeled round, grabbing Fizzgig, and fled through the window.

"Come back!" they heard the Skeksis begging them. "Kelffinks, no! Peace! Please! Peace!"

As they ran into the forest again, Jen turned his head to see whether the Skeksis was following them. It was not. It was simply watching them go, its head hanging in dejection.

Brian Froud

CHAPTER VI
TO THE CASTLE

Deep within the castle, in his laboratory known as the Chamber of Life, skekTek the Scientist sorted through a load of Pod People squirming together in a wicker cage. He pulled several out to inspect them more closely under a magnifying glass and tossed them back into the cage with a shake of his head.

Beside him, the Garthim-Master impatiently peered at each specimen and looked inquiringly at the Scientist. With each rejection, he bared his teeth and grunted in disappointment. He tried to help by pointing out likely candidates. The Scientist would glance briefly at each, then roll his eyes toward the ceiling with a dismissive flap of his hand. He was the specialist in this business. The Garthim-Master had no understanding of the mysteries of laboratory work.

Eventually, the Scientist found a specimen he thought might serve the purpose. Closing the top of the wicker cage to prevent the rest from escaping, the Scientist carried the wriggling peasant by one arm to a row of metal chairs fitted against the stone wall. He clamped his specimen into the chair by tightening a wormscrew. In a bracket at the front of the chair was a crystal to which a long glass tube was attached. The tube was slightly inclined, and beneath its lower extremity the Scientist placed a jeweled flask. Then he walked back to his control bench. The Garthim-Master watched, licking his lips eagerly and blinking. The peasant went on wriggling his limbs, but his head and torso were rigidly held. Only his black button eyes could swivel, in panic, and his mouth emit helpless little moans.

When the Scientist pulled a lever, a portal swung open in the wall opposite the clamped peasant. Behind the portal, a vertical shaft was revealed, down the center of which a continuous beam of energy, violet in color, was visible. At the far bottom of the shaft, deep within the planet's crust, the beam terminated in a lake of fire.

The Scientist, motioning the Garthim-Master to stand well clear of the area, pulled down another lever. A rod swung out from the side of the vertical shaft. To the end of it a prism of crystal was attached. The rod moved the prism into the beam of energy and held it there, refracting a violet ray across the laboratory into the peasant's face.

Immediately, the peasant stopped squirming and became rigid. From his fingertips, at the end of his extended arms, a crackling force field jumped to meet the crystal in front of the chair. There, it condensed into thick, oily droplets, which ran down the incline of the tube and dripped into the flask. The peasant's eyes were transformed from black buttons into milky, staring orbs. They remained like that when the Scientist reversed his levers, closing off the shaft again. The peasant's body, twitching, sagged limply in the clamped chair.

The Scientist retrieved the flask with the collected droplets and handed it to the Garthim-Master, who drank off its contents in one impatient gulp.

The vliya had an immediate impact on him. His wrinkles smoothed, his neck straightened, his whole bearing became more vigorous. He strutted across the laboratory to admire himself in a mirror, holding his body at different angles to take in the transformation.

As he watched, and preened, the effect drained away as rapidly as it had arrived. His skin sagged, his spine curved, his eyes became yellow. He turned accusingly to the Scientist, his mouth trembling with bitter anger.

The Scientist spread his hands and shrugged. The Garthim-Master knew as well as he what the problem was. They were all too dissipated for the Pod vliya, which was no more than sap, to have any lasting salutary effect on their flaccid flesh. There was nothing for it but to await the Great Conjunction, when they would derive a tremendously renewed power from the Crystal.

The Garthim-Master hurled the jeweled flask across the laboratory at the Scientist, who ducked. The flask smashed into a cabinet, on the shelves of which were laid out the maimed and dismembered bodies of all kinds of creatures. Some of them were still, morbidly, alive, but the Scientist was not worried that they would escape. In none of them remained the will to do so. Elsewhere in the laboratory, recently captured animals, still healthy until they had been subjected to the Scientist's experiments, were confined in cages or tethered to the floor.

The Garthim-Master stormed away. He had been depending on the Scientist, who, together with the Slave-Master, he had thought to be his chief support among the Skeksis. Now, without any assistance from the vliya, he would have to confront the Ritual-Master's dangerous challenge for the throne. Sooner or later, it would come to *Haakskeekah!* And, his pride humbled by his recent humiliation, the Garthim-Master lacked confidence in his will to win the next duel. How clever the Ritual-Master had been, to let his two rivals destroy themselves! His stratagem would not have worked if the Garthim had brought in the Gelfling. Twice the spy crystals had located those puny animalcules—first one of them, now a pair of the things—and twice the Garthim had utterly failed to capture them. Stupid Garthim! Stupid, stupid Garthim! Once the Garthim-Master's greatest pride, now his traitors.

When the Garthim-Master had left the Chamber of Life, the Scientist released the peasant from the chair and threw him aside. The peasant picked himself up and walked meekly across the floor to stand in line with the other newly created slaves. All their eyes were milky blanks.

In the wicker cage, the untreated Pod People continued to squirm over each other, crying haplessly. The Scientist looked at them and found them tedious. It would take him several hours to drain the vliya from this load, and the Garthim were waiting below, by the castle gate, with more of the creatures, brought in from the latest raid. They were next to useless now. The Skeksis had more than enough slaves for the time to come, but that time would be seriously curtailed if Pod sap were the only vliya they had.

He searched his laboratory with his eyes, hoping to discover some alternative source of bodily energy. The place was littered with the rotten fruits of his work since the last Great Conjunction. From all sorts of living beings, bones and flesh, marrow, filament, leaf, and tissue had been subjected to every torturous experiment the Scientist had been able to devise. He gazed skeptically at a retort full of Myrrhie fins he had steeped for weeks in two acids, distilling the resultant liquor. As soon as he had drunk it, he had become ill.

Aughra had cackled at that, the only sign of life she had shown from the cage where she was kept. The rest of the time she spent hunched in a brooding silence. Look at her now. Her eye, removed from its socket and sitting on a table, was beadily following him, as it always did, but the eye had taken on a life of its own, independent of the bloated body, slumped and sullen, it belonged to.

The Scientist began to calculate how he might extract elixir from Aughra's eye.

Kira knew where she was going. She darted along the paths of the forest, through brambles and thickets, as though she had spent all her life in the woodlands rehearsing for the day when she would have to escape from a Skeksis.

"Is this the way to the castle?" Jen asked, panting.

"It's not the most direct way," she replied. "In fact, we've been heading in exactly the opposite direction all day. But it will turn out to be the quickest. You'll see."

"I hope you're right," Jen said. "Have you seen the suns today? They looked as though they were going to touch."

"Yes," Kira said. "It's a strange light, isn't it? I suppose it means we're approaching this Great Conjunction Aughra told you about."

"I'm sure it does. And everything I do seems to depend upon getting to the castle by the time that happens."

"Don't fret," Kira told him. "You'll see."

Where the forest started to thin out again, the land became undulating. Jen and Kira found themselves running down hills so precipitous that they had to traverse, and then to do the same again to climb the next rise. Still, Kira knew the way, always found the trodden path. The Pod People had occasionally brought her this far abroad on their expeditions, she explained, when at certain seasons of the year there were rare fruits and nuts to be found for those who knew the isolated tree.

They came to a flowery lea where the large undulations settled down into a range of low hillocks. There, Kira halted at last. Jen was glad of the rest. He was more winded than she was. His upbringing in the valley of the urRu had never required sustained effort of this sort. He had seldom had to travel as far as a thousand paces. Kira was obviously quite used to it.

Now, she was standing on top of a hillock, uttering a strange string of chirps and clicks, like an insect in the hot weather.

"What are you doing?" Jen asked.

"Ssssh!" She raised a finger to her lips, then pointed with a small chuckle of pleasure.

Toward them over the hillocks four catlike beasts, three of them fully grown and one a cub, came galloping on long, stiff legs. Rangy in action, creamy in color, with long whiskers, they were like no animal Jen had ever known.

"Landstriders!" Kira called in delighted welcome. She turned to Jen, who was looking unnerved. "Don't be afraid," she said. "They'll take us wherever I ask them to. They *hate* the Skeksis. And the Garthim—they *fight!*"

"You don't have to come with me," Jen told her.

She looked at him for a long time. "I know," she replied quietly.

Followed by Fizzgig who was putting up his usual bold show behind her ankles, she went to talk quietly to the Landstriders. At once, hearing her request, they became frisky.

Kira beckoned to Jen. As he approached, he realized just how large the adult Landstriders were and how high off the ground he would be when seated on one.

The Landstriders docilely walked to the side of the steep little hummock, from the top of which Kira climbed onto one of them. Fizzgig, left on the ground, set up an incredible commotion when he saw that he was not going on the journey. Roaring, he bounced up and down beside Kira's Landstrider, higher and higher with each bounce.

"No," Kira said to him, "not you, little big mouth."

Fizzgig redoubled his racket, bouncing so high that at the peak of his bounce he was level with Kira.

Relenting, she laughed and grabbed him out of the air. "All right," she said. Fizzgig nestled down contentedly inside her pouch. Then Kira turned to Jen. "Choose your Landstrider."

Jen looked at her face. It was quite lovely suffused with elation.

He chose the slightly smaller of the two remaining adults and, under Kira's guidance, struggled onto its back and leaned forward, clutching the animal's neck.

"Hold on tight!" Kira cried.

She clicked her tongue, and with a dizzying surge of power beneath him Jen felt his arms tugged straight. A wind was humming past his ears, and his hair was streaming behind him.

At first, he bounced around on the Landstrider's back. It was extremely uncomfortable at best, and at worst he thought he might crash down to the ground far below him. Gradually, he and the Landstrider worked out a reciprocal rhythm, and after that the ride was sheer joy. As for Kira, the modest reserve of her normal manner had vanished. She was whooping and shrieking.

"Hold on very tight, Jen!" she laughed.

He could only nod. Their speed was breathtaking. The trees along the margin of the forest were a blurred palisade. His ears were filled with the wind and the drumming of the Landstriders' paws on the turf. Small animals dashed out of their way, and leaves flew up where the riders passed. Jen had no time to consider whether his arm, still bound in green moss, was hurting him.

Brian Froud

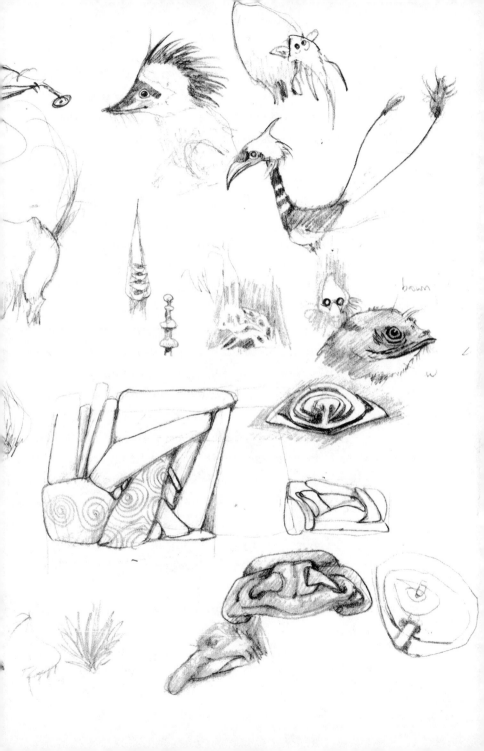

brown

The Landstriders never faltered in their pace. Around the forest margins they carried the Gelfling, and then across a wide plain, through a powdery crater, up and down hills, along ravines, and twice they leaped the black river, sinuous across the landscape.

Beside the higher reaches of the black river, near the swamp, the weary trek of the urRu progressed. UrZah, leading the long, dusty, plodding file, leaned on his stick and slowly turned his great neck to gaze into the sky. The three suns stood in equilateral triangulation. UrZah lowered his head again and slouched on, toward the castle, toward a birth or a death.

At length the Landstriders bounded to the crest of a hill, and there Kira pulled up, calling to Jen to do likewise. With tongue clicks she gentled the Landstriders who were still eager to sprint onward.

Jen and Kira were awed by the view that lay before them. At the foot of the long rocky incline below was the castle entrance, a tube bridging a deep ravine. The massive bulk of the fortress itself towered up much higher than the hilltop where they stood. To see the craggy battlements, stark against the sky, they had to crane their necks although they were still some distance away. The immensity was dramatized by the ravine, which apparently ran all the way around the base of the castle buildings. To their right, the ravine was a sheer drop below the castle wall. The stronghold of the Skeksis was colossal, black and malign, forbidding as the rock from which it had been hewn.

Kira pointed down to the castle entrance. "Look!"

Jen looked. "Garthim."

"Yes," Kira replied. "But can you see what one of them is carrying?"

Jen strained to see. He could make out a round object of some sort.

"It's one of those wicker cages in which they put their prisoners," Kira said. "Don't you think so?"

"I can't tell from here," Jen answered. "But if you're right, it will be your own villagers in there."

The Landstriders were pawing the ground and growling deeply. Jen's was already edging forward, unable to contain impatience.

Kira clicked her tongue again, and the Landstriders bounded keenly down the slope. They were going full speed as they closed on the Garthim. Then they hit.

To deliver their assault, they had to spring from their hind legs so as to drive their front ones into the hated foe. The effect on Jen and Kira was that, on impact, their momentum threw them off their mounts and they rolled free, past the line of bristling Garthim. Fizzgig went with them.

While Landstriders and Garthim grappled with a deafening roar and clash, Jen and Kira picked themselves up. Jen was looking at the castle entrance, ready to sprint inside, but Kira's first thought was for the cage they had seen. The impact of the Landstriders had knocked it from the Garthim's grasp. It had bounced and rolled toward the ravine, and came to a stop on the brink.

Kira ran across to it. She had been right. Pod People were packed closely inside. Hands protruded, beseechingly.

Kira shouted, "Jen!" as she began to tear at the cage. Inside, her face crushed and contorted against the wicker bars, was Ydra. "Don't worry," Kira was saying, "don't worry. We'll get you out of there, Ydra! We'll get you all out!" Kira's fingers scrabbled helplessly at the metal fastenings of the lid of the cage.

Jen raced to help her. The wicker bars were jointed together with leather thongs. He twisted with his fingers and Kira tried biting with her teeth, but it took them some time to undo one thong. The loosened bar now allowed only one peasant to squeeze through with difficulty and escape. There were probably twenty Pod People crammed inside. Jen took out the shard and used it on another thong, glancing anxiously behind him.

The Landstriders were magnificent, but their fight was doomed. One of them was rolling on the ground, wrestling with a Garthim, while the other was invisible beneath a pile of black carapaces. Two Garthim were not engaged in the battle, seeming to hesitate between attacking one of the Landstriders and pursuing the Gelfling.

With renewed frenzy Jen slashed at the thong, hoping against hope. If the shard could cut through this one, he ought to be able to release Ydra, who was moaning right in front of him.

Behind him, in the din, he heard a clattering, snarling noise growing closer. He threw a glance over his shoulder and screamed to Kira. Both of them jumped, in opposite directions, as the wrestling, growling ball of locked Landstrider and Garthim rolled over and over toward them and plummeted down the ravine to smash on the rocks far below.

Jen was staring down the precipice with horror when he heard Kira shout. He looked up. Four Garthim were about to converge on them. There was no escape route past them toward the hill, and the way along the ravine's edge to the bridge was also blocked off.

Jen stepped in front of Kira, holding the shard out like a dagger. Fizzgig was whimpering on her shoulder. Behind the Garthim, the remaining Landstrider was on its back, still mauling and clawing but near the end of its fight.

The Gelfling stood on the edge of the precipice. As the black Garthim loomed over them, tentacles groping out for them, Jen felt Kira wrap her arms tightly around his waist from behind him. Then he was pulled over backward by her. His mouth gaped with shock as they toppled over the edge.

They were not dropping but floating, fluttering like sycamore wings through the air.

Still held firmly in Kira's arms, Jen twisted his neck to see where the bottom of the ravine was, thinking that perhaps it always felt like this, that the mind stretched out the last fleeting moments of life beyond their time.

He saw that they still had some way to fall and that what they were floating on was a pair of diaphanous wings, which had unfolded from Kira's back.

He looked up to the top of the ravine. Silhouetted against the sky, the Garthim were milling about aimlessly on the edge of the precipice.

Jen and Kira, with Fizzgig still on her shoulder, landed gently at the bottom of the ravine.

"How did you do that?" Jen asked as they stood up again.

"Don't you know?" Kira replied. "Once, ages ago," she explained, "we Gelfling could really fly, not just flutter down like that." She looked quizzically at him. "Didn't the urRu teach you anything useful?"

"But I don't have wings!" Jen insisted.

Kira smiled. "Of course not. You're a boy!"

She looked around. The gully of the ravine was a noisome place, littered with the trash and ordure that the Skeksis had jettisoned there over time. Near them lay the broken bodies of the Landstrider and Garthim still entwined like fatal lovers. The tentacles on the Garthim and its legs, ending in plated, round feet, were very slowly twitching in the air. It was, no doubt, the nervous system making its last pact with death, but Jen jumped when he saw it and moved away, unsure whether a Garthim could die.

Kira put her hand in Jen's, and they walked cautiously along the defile, curving around the base of the sheer cliff walls below the castle. They were slowly gaining height, but Jen wondered whether they would ever find their way up from the ravine to the castle entrance. And what they would do there, faced with the Garthim, was another question.

Even down here, he doubted whether they were safe from the Garthim. The Skeksis surely must know by now that the Gelfling had reached the castle. If there was a way of sending Garthim down here to catch them, they would be sent, assuming—Jen allowed himself a spark of hope—assuming, that was, that the Garthim were able to transmit information to the Skeksis. If not, then the Skeksis would be depending on a fresh reconnaissance by the spy-crystal bats. That would surely allow for a brief breathing space. Jen glanced up at the sky. He saw nothing there yet. It was even possible, he reflected, that the Skeksis did not know that the Gelfling were in the vicinity. Possibly the Skeksis' only means of knowing their location would have been if one of them, alerted by the noise of fighting, had looked out from the castle toward the gate and seen Kira and himself before they went over the edge of the ravine.

Having little else on which to build his hopes, Jen decided to believe that, for the moment, Kira and he did have the advantage of surprise. A small advantage it was, considering the balance of forces against them. But to believe in it was better than to despair.

Following the curve of the cliff, around a buttress of rock, they came to the start of what seemed to be a long carving in the rock face. Farther on, foul water was trickling down. The carving continued, Jen could see, beyond the foul-water outlet.

And then he realized that the carving his hand rested on was of a great tooth. Next to it was another tooth, and another.

He stood away from the rock wall to take in the entire carving. Glaring out from the rock was the face of a gargoyle, with bulging eyes and beetled brow. Its mouth gaped open, and from the mouth came the trickle of foul water.

Moving on, heart pounding, to stand directly in front of the gargoyle, Jen could see a black tunnel stretching away into the rock pile.

He remembered what the Skeksis at the Gelfling ruins had offered: "Show you way into castle with me, secret way, no Garthim see, through Teeth of Shkreesh."

Jen turned to Kira, trying to keep from his voice the loathing he felt for what had to be done. "This is our way into the castle," he told her.

She nodded, shuddering. Simply to climb into that vomitory was appalling enough as an idea, even without the fetid tunnel behind it to negotiate, and then what awaited them in the castle itself.

"There's no other way," Jen said apologetically.

"I know."

He spread his hands. "And I can't leave you here. Because that would be even more dangerous."

"You can't leave me here," Kira said, "because I am not going to be left anywhere."

Jen nodded, accepting the rebuke.

First Jen, and then Kira with Fizzgig, climbed through the Teeth of Shkreesh. The Chamberlain, watching them from the top of the ravine, smiled, and stealthily turned away into the castle.

Large
cloak
pin

Brian Froud

CHAPTER VII
INTO THE DARK

The tunnel was coated with slime. Perhaps the source of the faint light was the luminescence of decay, or it was simply the light from the ravine exit reflected endlessly up the shining, putrid tube. Had Jen and Kira been able to hold their breath indefinitely, they would have done so. As it was, the urge to retch did not abate until their senses took pity and adjusted to the rancid air.

They were clambering upward; the passageway inclined quite steeply at times. There were so many bends that they had soon lost all sense of direction. That did not matter; they had no real choices. The tunnel's only features were ulcerous alcoves here and there, clusters of stalactites, and the rustling and slithering of creatures who had their abode in this foul passage. In the dim light, the Gelfling glimpsed a smooth white snake watching them, a colony of crested lice, and a creature resembling an elongated frog, with fur round its face and two large, glowing saucerlike eyes. Fizzgig was so frightened of these apparitions that he dared not even growl at them; instead, with an anxious little grunting noise, he scuttled at Kira's heels.

As they penetrated deeper into the tunnel, its character began to alter. They noticed several side tunnels and branching conduits in the roof, all of them small and evidently not routes to the heart of the castle and the Crystal. But shortly afterward, they came to a junction where the main tunnel split off into three directions.

"Which way do you think?" Jen asked.

"Which route to death?" Kira rejoined. "I smell death here."

"Don't despair now," Jen said. "We've gotten this far because of your courage. I'd have stayed in the forest."

"No, you wouldn't have. I always knew your quest would bring you here. It was you who forgot it for a while."

"It's too late to go back now."

"I know. I didn't really think of it. It's just that this place…"

Jen studied the three tunnels for some sort of clue, but found none. All three were oval, mucid underfoot, dripping with a hollow echo. He shrugged and took out the shard. Holding the palm of one hand flat, he balanced the shard on it and waited to see if anything would happen. The shard glowed softly and stirred in his hand. It moved around, like a compass needle, to point toward the middle tunnel of the three.

"That's the one we'll take," Jen said.

The ceiling got higher as they advanced along the tunnel. The slime graduated into soil, and the walls became bare rock. Wooden beams in the roof were evidence of occupation. The ground was impacted hard, perhaps by Garthim feet. Jen and Kira continued their upward climb but on a gently rising slope, and the improving light allowed them to see farther ahead.

Jen's heart was beating faster. Soon, they would be entering the castle itself, and then he would have no guidance. He would have to rely on his intuition. Would it be obvious where the Crystal was?

Would it not be guarded? Perhaps not—if the Skeksis were ignorant of the Gelfling presence in the castle, then they would have no reason to guard it. Suppose he succeeded in restoring the shard, what then? Would the Skeksis be rendered powerless on the spot, unable to punish him?

Just before them, a shadow fell across their path. They froze.

From an alcove, the Chamberlain stepped out. His bulk completely filled the tunnel. He was so close to them that the stench of his breath caused them to recoil. Before they could turn and retreat, he had seized them, one in each bony hand. Fizzgig leaped from Kira and crouched at the side of the tunnel, yelping desperately.

The Chamberlain had a smile on his face. "Knew you come," he said. "Please, not be afraid. Am here to help you. We make peace now, little Kelffinks and Skeksis, yes."

"No!" Kira cried.

The Skeksis was grasping them too firmly for them to escape, but he did not do what they knew he could—simply strangle the life from them, as the life had been strangled from Kira's mother years ago. It was clear that he wanted something from them other than their deaths.

"Please, you come with me now?" the Chamberlain was asking them. "Yes Kelffinks live with Skeksis together in peace, yes. Please."

Jen's arms were free enough, within the grip of the Skeksis, for him to slide a hand inside his tunic and take hold of the shard.

"We go now," the Chamberlain said, starting to drag them up the tunnel, "or it be too late. Please."

In one rapid movement, Jen drew out the shard and with both hands plunged it into the Chamberlain's arm.

The shard gave off a blinding flash. The tunnel rumbled as small stones fell down from the roof.

In the wilderness on the horizon, urSol the Chanter held up his arm. A deep gash had suddenly appeared in it, freshly bleeding. The file of the urRu trekked on toward the castle. In the sky above them, the three suns were drawing closer to each other.

With a thunderous snarl, the Chamberlain, momentarily stunned by pain, released Jen. His other arm still clutched Kira. Before Jen could try to release her, too, the Chamberlain had used his wounded arm to knock him to the ground. As he tumbled, Jen kept a tight grip on the shard, instinctively shielding it from the Skeksis. Then the Chamberlain reached up, gripped a supporting beam in the roof of the tunnel, and dragged it downward. The roof caved in, and Jen collapsed beneath an avalanche of stone and soil.

As Kira was carried away up the tunnel, she looked back in horror at the pile of rubble that had buried Jen. Fizzgig, whimpering, was bouncing loyally after her.

"No, Fizzgig!" Kira cried out. "No! Go back! Stay with Jen! Stay with Jen, Fizzgig!"

Fizzgig reluctantly obeyed, standing still as he watched Kira, writhing in the Chamberlain's clutch, disappear at the end of the tunnel.

The Garthim-Master sat unusually alert upon his throne. Here was the opportunity to outwit the Ritual-Master for good and to enter a golden age of imperial rule, after the tremendous reinforcement of their power that the Skeksis would derive from the Great Conjunction. He must not make any mistakes this time.

Consider: A Gelfling, apprehended by the Chamberlain, whom everyone had supposed to be wandering forever in the outer wilderness. A live Gelfling! The only species that could ever threaten the dominion of the Skeksis, according to the old prophecy concerning the restoration of the crystal shard—the species had therefore been liquidated. The Garthim-Master suppressed the superstitious shiver that even now ran through him at the thought of Gelfling. The Chamberlain would have to be given credit for his captive, if only to dissuade him from crowing about his success where the Garthim-Master's Garthim had twice failed. But not too much credit. Praise him for his Gelfling, then ask him what had happened to the other Gelfling reported by the spy crystals. That would catch him off-balance. Then restore him to his office of Chamberlain, the second minister of the castle. Accept his homage. Next: The Ritual-Master. He had no grounds now for issuing a challenge to *Haakskeekah!* The Gelfling menace was being contained under the Garthim-Master's Emperorship. To argue that it had been contained despite the Garthim-Master's failure with his Garthim would, in the atmosphere of celebration and imminent conjunction, simply be petty. It was true that pettiness was a strong suit among the Skeksis, but the Ritual-Master had always affected to be above such sentiments, ostentatiously devoting himself to a life of hypocritical piety. So what course would he take now? He would want to make the most of this Gelfling for his own purposes: ritual sacrifice. He fancied himself to be at his best when rabid cruelty and high ceremony were mixed. He would have to be preempted, and the Scientist was the answer. The Scientist had to be instructed to requisition the Gelfling for his laboratory, in which case the Ritual-Master would not be able to argue that the claims of ritual preceded the claims of research and security. The Garthim-Master would offer the Scientist the opportunity to dissect a Gelfling in search of a means to eradicate the creatures forever. The Garthim-Master frowned. Until now they all had supposed that the Gelfling already had been exterminated. It was a mystery where these two new ones had sprung from. Spontaneous generation, perhaps? The Scientist would have to find a way to prevent that in the future. Should his advice be to destroy all life, both sentient and inanimate, outside the castle, so be it. For their own sustenance, they could breed Nebrie in the dungeons, and allow the Garthim to pillage and kill all over the globe. That would always leave the urRu, of course. The Skeksis could not destroy them. But the urRu were, by definition, no threat to the Skeksis any more than the mirror was a threat to the face. So that left the way clear for the Garthim-Master to accomplish his two most cherished ambitions: he would always sit on this throne; and, with the Scientist's connivance, he would drink this Gelfling's vliya and that other Gelfling's as well, when it was found. And then let the Ritual-Master do what he could.

To the hosannas of the milky-eyed Pod choir, the ragged Chamberlain swaggered into the Throne Room with Kira clutched in his claws, held above his head. The other Skeksis, drawn up in two lines, could not forbear to lean forward and examine the little creature in curiosity and scarcely controlled apprehension. Since the moment the Ornamentalist had rushed in, babbling about a Gelfling and the Chamberlain, they had been waiting agog. Now, here it was, a living example of the only virus that might prevent the renewal of their power: located, trapped, safe.

The Chamberlain made a profound obeisance to his all-wise Emperor. Holding Kira out before him, offering her to the throne, he embarked on a rapid recital of how subtly and persistently he had pursued and overtaken her. He would have gone on to a chilling description of the Skeksis' fate without his enterprise had the Ritual-Master not interrupted.

"*Kelffink Krakweekah!*" the Ritual-Master screeched. At the same time, he pointed at Kira and drew his talons across his throat, making his meaning quite clear.

The Ritual-Master had made but one step forward, intending to take due possession of his sacrificial victim, when the Garthim-Master, raising his scepter bellowed a denial.

Remaining where he was, the Ritual-Master nevertheless drew out the long, brilliant blade of his sacrificial knife. He held it and stared at the Garthim-Master. The pose was one that the Garthim-Master did not find ambiguous.

The Chamberlain, meanwhile, was issuing his own protest. The Gelfling was his prisoner, and what was to be done with it should be his decision.

Beckoning the Scientist to him for a private consultation, the Garthim-Master talked quietly to him, and the Scientist nodded decisively several times.

Then the Garthim-Master addressed the assembly. "*Kelffink na Rakhash,*" he declared.

Not all the Skeksis were in agreement with the proclamation. Some doubted the Scientist's effectiveness in his Chamber of Life. The Ornamentalist was devising uses for Kira's severed head. The Gourmand was savoring thoughts of the rest of her body. And all of them knew perfectly well where the Garthim-Master's interest lay. Probably it was a deficiency of Gelfling vliya that had killed the old Emperor. Now, if the Scientist could have designed a completely safe method of breeding Gelfling in captivity, with a regular production of vliya, they would have saluted him. Indeed, that would have given him a direct route to the throne. But, as the Ritual-Master was even now screeching to the assembly, the Scientist was a mere Pod processor, a self-mutilating crank. Would it not be more fitting to celebrate their

Jim Henson's Creature Shop

salvation, the Ritual-Master demanded, by use of this ceremonial knife he was holding?

The Garthim-Master did not like the way things were going. He himself did not hold much respect for the Scientist, but he had assumed that the others did. Which of *them* would have severed their own limbs for the sake of pure, disinterested enquiry?

Still, disagreement persisted, and the Ritual-Master continued pressing his bloodthirsty intention.

The Garthim-Master realized that he had to change his tactics. He muttered confidentially again to the Scientist, who was unmoved by the whole fracas, then strode down from the throne to take possession of the Gelfling.

Holding her aloft, he declared portentously, "*Kelffink cho tenkha. Vo olk Kelffink ulls?*"

The other Gelfling? In their excitement at seeing this one, several Skeksis had given no thought to the other one. There was consternation, from which the Garthim-Master profited by passing Kira quietly to the Scientist, who made off with her to his Chamber of Life. Eyes turned to the Chamberlain. Where, indeed, was the other Gelfling?

This was the Chamberlain's trump card. He explained coolly. The Gelfling he had just brought in to them was the one that had spent all this time concealed among the Pod People. It was not inexplicable that it had eluded detection by the spy crystals. Gelfling and Pod People were, after all, of similar size. The other Gelfling which had appeared at Aughra's Observatory from an unknown origin, was no longer a risk to them. The Chamberlain had made certain of that. He did feel, however, that he could not justify producing the other Gelfling's body for them until he was assured that he himself was restored to a secure position within the Skeksis hierarchy. Alive or dead, a Gelfling's body was, they all knew, an object of rare value. Were he not welcome back in the castle, with all his previous honors and powers returned, he might prefer to retain sole possession of the body and savor the vliya himself.

The Garthim-Master raised his scepter once more, and ordered the Ornamentalist to fetch the Chamberlain's robes and insignia. Praising the Chamberlain for his selfless devotion to the well-being of the Skeksis state, the Garthim-Master commanded the Ritual-Master to robe their returned brother in all his former raiment. The Ritual-Master, hissing, resentfully complied, seeing no alternative for the present. While the robing was in progress, the Garthim-Master held his scepter ceremonially over the bowed head of the Chamberlain and duly readmitted him to his official position. The other Skeksis uttered cries of harsh salute.

The Chamberlain knelt in homage. The Garthim-Master bent gravely over him, with the scepter aloft, and murmured in his ear: Where is the other Gelfling?

The Chamberlain told him.

The Garthim-Master nodded. The two of them would go for it themselves, he muttered. Rather that than trust the Garthim.

As the two of them rose and strutted in pomp from the chamber, cries of homage rang in their ears.

In the tunnel, Fizzgig had been sniffing at the pile of rubble. He began to dig, but it took a long time for his small, rubbery paws to make any impression. After much work, he had uncovered one of Jen's hands. He sniffed at it, licked it, and even gently nibbled the fingers, to provoke life. The hand did not move.

Fizzgig sat down again and kept guard.

The Scientist's hands were trembling with excitement as he clamped Kira into the chair on the wall of his laboratory. Fumbling, he half dropped her once but snatched her up before she hit the floor. It was not only the satisfaction of extracting the true Gelfling vliya again, after years of Pod sap, that was agitating him. He also knew that the Garthim-Master would not remember the exact amount of vliya a Gelfling could yield. But the Scientist did remember and was confident that he could cache a large portion of it without being discovered. He glanced at Aughra in her cage. He did not trust her. Given the chance, she would have informed on him out of spite. But she seemed scarcely awake now. She had tried to bite him when he had taken her eye, the malicious old hag. Since then, she had been squatting in a silent huddle. He had placed her eye on his workbench but had not yet decided what to do with it.

Controlling himself, he fitted the crystal and inclined glass tube into its bracket, beneath which he placed a large collecting jar. From it he could decant the vliya into the jeweled flask for the Garthim-Master, and the rest of it would be his.

He went to his controls and pulled the levers.

The violet ray penetrated Kira's eyes, which began to cloud over more gradually than Pod eyes did, as the force field crackled from her fingers to the crystal in front of her. The precious, viscous droplets started to run down the tube and drip into the collecting jar. Unlike Kira's eyes, those of the Scientist were aglow.

Struggling in the chair, Kira called out, "Jen! Help me!"

The agony in her cry reached Jen, although he was too far away to hear her voice. Beneath the pile of rubble, he stirred and groaned. The weight on his back was crushing him. With his mouth pressed on rock, he called out, "Kira! Fight them!"

Fizzgig was alerted. He tried digging again, frantically, but was discouraged by the minimal effect he was having. Sadly, he licked Jen's fingers.

The rasp of Fizzgig's tongue was the first indication Jen had that he was not totally interred. He wriggled his fingers, then tried flexing his arm that had the moss still bound to it. The rubble shifted, then sloughed off.

With his free arm, Jen could grope blindly at pieces of rock, and, once grasping them, throw them off himself. The effort made him grunt, but with each chunk that he removed he was able to breathe more easily. Once his head was free, he leaned on his arm and levered his body against it. More rubble slipped down from his back, allowing him to kneel upright and use both hands. Fizzgig was in ecstasies of barking.

Jen had started to clear his legs when Fizzgig stopped barking and instead set up a low growl. By this time Jen thought he understood Fizzgig's language. "Ssssh!" he said and listened keenly.

From farther up the tunnel he heard the sound of heavy bodies approaching and the hiss of their breathing.

With a last effort and a wince of pain, he straightened his knees and the remaining rubble ran off. He felt dizzy, but his body still worked.

"Ssssh!" he repeated to Fizzgig.

Painfully, Jen ran on tiptoe back down the tunnel. When he reached the junction where the tunnel split off he doubled back up a different branch. Fizzgig stayed with him and remained blissfully silent.

"Jen! Jen!" Kira called out again, transfixed by the violet ray. Her eyes were burning, her body felt like lead. What power of will remained to her derived from anger at what was being done to her. She fought to keep her anger blazing. Once that had left her, she knew she would have left herself. And then Jen's fervent exhortation to "Fight them!" traveled back to her, and her courage rose. The milky film over her eyes started to recede.

She heard a voice calling to her across the Chamber of Life. It was an old woman's voice.

"Gelfling," Aughra croaked. Her eye, though removed to the Scientist's bench, was watching Kira. "Call on those around you, in this place. Help you, they can, if you call on them. You are Gelfling, you have powers of Gelfling. Use them. Speak to those who are here with you. Stronger than Skeksis, they are, all together, if you can speak to them. You can."

Kira concentrated all her strength into focusing her dazzled eyes. In the gloom beyond the ray, she could make out cabinets and cages, but it was impossible for her to identify the morbid shapes lying there.

In all the tongues of the animals of the wild, learned and practiced throughout her childhood, she cried out. She cried for help, she cried for freedom.

Around the room, there was a rustling, a stirring. For the first time in many years, the voices of the captive and drained animals began to speak in the Chamber of Life. First one started to trill, then another was barking, and others took up the refrain. In a swelling chorus, more and more prisoners answered Kira's cry.

The Scientist was startled. Looking anxiously about, he picked up a stick and scuttled around, banging on bars and doors, hissing threats. It made no difference. A sweet cacophony of screeches, yelps, hoots, squawks, and roars rang out. Bodies were moving now, rattling their prisons, louder and louder. "Yes, Gelfling, yes, yes. All together, they can be free. Oh, yes!"

Kira, hope fluttering in her throat, redoubled her cries.

The Scientist, coming to his senses, attacked the root of the problem. He crossed the laboratory and put his gray, scaly, clawed hand across Kira's mouth. She bit with all her might. Now his cry of pain was added to the concert.

Under the combined assault of a multitude of creatures, cage doors were springing open. First singly, then in scores, the prisoners were breaking out, and the maimed were recovering some strength. All of them made it their first task to attack the Scientist. Their wills, their dignities, which he assumed had been cauterized, were reawakened when their names were called, their languages spoken to them.

Birds flew up and flapped in the Scientist's face. He staggered, in vain waving his hands to get rid of them. He stumbled on animals milling around his feet. In his ears was the cackle of Aughra. Off-balance and half blinded by a coronet of birds, he lunged vengefully in her direction. Missing Aughra's cage, he crashed into the open portal, knocking askew the rod with the crystal prism.

As the violet ray beamed off Kira's face, the Scientist teetered on the brink of the portal, then dropped down the vertical shaft into the lake of fire far below.

Trekking through the wilderness, across the powdery crater, the long, weary file of the urRu saw urTih the Alchemist suddenly burst into flames. Within seconds, he was reduced to a pile of ashes.

"Tell them release you," Aughra said.

Kira spoke to the animals. With beaks and claws they untwisted the wormscrew of the clamp. Kira fell to the ground.

Aughra gestured in the direction of the collecting jar. "Drink that stuff," she told Kira. "Yours, it is."

Kira picked up the jar and drank the vliya. In the mirror she saw a blurred image of herself. As she watched, the image became sharper. Her eyes had quite lost the milkiness that had filmed them. She started to feel stronger, though dazed. But when the vliya had completed its work, not all the effects of her ordeal had been reversed. The skin around her eyes and mouth remained lines, and her hair was paler in color. She looked older than she had.

Aughra was still squatting in her cage. "You see my eye?" she asked. "Up on that bench?"

"How can you see where it is with no eyes?" Kira asked her.

"Can't. But it can see where it is, can't it?"

Kira picked up the eye delicately and, stepping through the flocks of rioting animals, went to open Aughra's cage. She handed Aughra her eye.

Aughra screwed it back into its socket and squinted up at Kira. "Good Gelfling," she said. "But"—she shook her head—"you not the one with shard."

"No," Kira acknowledged. "What do you know about the shard?"

"My shard," Aughra said with a little pride. "What you know?"

"Jen has it." Kira was finding it hard to think straight. Her mind was still numbed. "Aren't you coming out of that cage?" she asked.

"Do for now," Aughra replied. "This Jen, where he, huh?"

"We were in a tunnel. He was buried by a fall of rock. He might be dead."

Aughra clicked her tongue. "Tsk-tsk. Too late, then."

"Too late for what?" Kira asked, trying to remember what she was doing here at all.

"Oh." Aughra shook her gray head. "Not know prophecy? Such

power for Skeksis soon, power over the stars. No one fight them, then. See suns? In sky? Soon, huh?"

"I've got to find Jen," Kira said. "Do you know the way to the tunnel?"

In reply, Aughra merely sucked her teeth.

Kira looked around in anguish. Then, still dazed, she ran through the doorway of the Chamber of Life and along any passages that promised to lead upward. She found herself running across a gallery that overlooked a triangular chamber. Below, she saw several Skeksis. She ducked beneath the balustrade. Skeksis, Garthim, whatever she met would now certainly destroy her on sight. But unless she could find Jen, it was all finished anyway.

From beneath the balustrade, something above the chamber caught her eye. She gasped. She was looking at a gigantic dark crystal, suspended in air.

From her cage, amid the chaos of freedom, Aughra watched Kira run out. "Go, Gelfling," she muttered to herself. "Go find your friend. Go find your death."

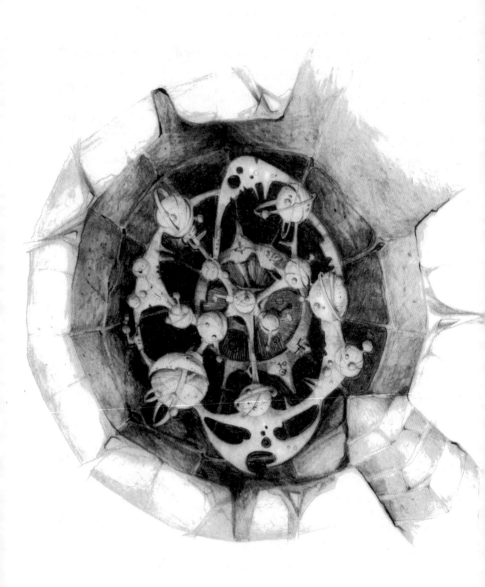

Jim Henson's Creature Shop

CHAPTER VIII
THE FIRE BELOW

Jen was gripping the shard so tightly that his knuckles were white and his wrist ached. He would do it, he *would* accomplish what he had come here to do, and he would not surrender to despair, that deathly face that beckoned so comfortingly to him. He would set aside his fear. And, hardest of all, he would not be discouraged by thinking of Kira's fate. There was nothing, he told himself, nothing he could do for Kira now. Were she here, she would be urging him to concentrate solely on restoring the shard. He gripped it even more tightly and swore that that was what he would do. For her, be she dead or, miraculously, still living.

Behind him, as he trod stealthily along the new tunnel, Fizzgig had started to bounce and squeal again. "Quiet," Jen said, turning to him. "We must be quiet, Fizzgig. Ssssh!"

Jen turned and took another step forward. As his foot landed, the ground gave way beneath it. Reaching out desperately for something to cling to, he found nothing. He plummeted down through a hatchway and landed on an earthen floor.

His body was so battered by now that he gave little thought to additional bruises. His only concern was whether he had disabled himself. He stood up, testing his limbs, and they seemed no worse than before. What was worse was his situation. Fizzgig was looking down at him from the open hatchway above, and Jen could see it was too high for him to jump back up. Was there some other way out of this pit? It was coal-black except for the exiguous light from the hatchway—and, Jen noticed, a mild glow from the shard. Was this the effect of bringing the shard into proximity with its mother crystal somewhere in this vast castle?

He held the shard up above his head like a faint torch. It enabled him barely to descry huge dark shapes around the walls of the pit.

And then an ominous clicking noise started up. By the shard's glow, Jen could see purple eyes switch open in the darkness. The clicking quickly accelerated, growing louder, and the entire Garthim pit came to life. The recently returned raiding party, instructed to seek out and destroy Gelfling, had been reactivated by the shard; and now each one of them lurched into motion, descending upon Jen, their claws snapping at him.

He had no time to think, to plan; nowhere to run. His actions were dictated by a blind surge of self-preservation. Holding the shard out before him as though it were a saber, and venting a wild yell of determination, he charged at the nearest of the Garthim.

Two of them simultaneously lunged at him. As he stopped short, they cannoned into each other, rebounding with a thunderous clang. Jen dodged them as they parted and attempted to pursue him. But the two Garthim were off-balance and, colliding again, they collapsed on top of each other.

Swift annihilators out in the open, the Garthim were clumsy and ineffectual in the confined space of their own pit. The two bodies on the floor, struggling with each other in an attempt to rise, brought down others that wanted to swarm over them to seize the Gelfling.

Jen, meanwhile, had come to a wall at the far end of the pit. He could see no door in it. The only exit seemed to be the hatchway he had fallen through, and there was no hope of reaching that. "Once, ages ago, we Gelfling could really fly," Kira had told him. But no more. He clutched the shard.

A huge claw swung at him, snapping shut. Jen ducked, and, though it missed his flesh, it closed on the back of his tunic. The claw swung out again, taking Jen off his feet and whirling him into the air. His tunic ripped, and he flew across the pit, yelling, thrusting out his free hand for anything he could grab on to in order to stay his fall.

He landed on the back of a Garthim and seized hold of some antenna like thing sprouting from its head. The Garthim reacted violently, weaving and twisting to shake this Gelfling off its back or to wrap a claw around it. Jen stabbed at its eyes with his shard, and one of them went out. The shard emitted a rich resonance and seemed to glow more brightly.

Other Garthim were swarming in on the one to which Jen clung. There were too many of them. They collided and trampled over each other, and such blows as they could deliver rained down on the Garthim beneath the Gelfling.

One mighty swipe missed completely and hammered into the wall of the pit. The tremendous force broke off a chunk of rock, leaving a hole through which a dim light filtered. Jen realized that a fissure had been made to somewhere outside, somewhere he did not know but somewhere that was not the Garthim pit. Leaping from the monster's back to the cleft, Jen hung there, one hand gripping the sharp new ledge. The other hand was still holding the shard; he thrust it back into his ripped tunic and clung to the ledge with two hands.

Garthim had wheeled and were converging on him. He dragged himself up onto the ledge and found he could twist his head and shoulders through the fissure.

What he saw on the other side of the fissure was a wide and very high vertical shaft. At its foot, so far below that it seemed halfway through the planet, there was fire, bubbling and crepitating. In the rough rock walls were ledges that might offer him some hope of climbing the shaft. A claw snapped behind his feet. He had no choice. Holding on to the friable rock curtain beside his head, he wriggled his body rapidly through the fissure and found a narrow ledge for his feet. Behind the fissure, the barrage of fierce hammering sounded like a volcano erupting. The rock wall on which Jen dangled was reverberating.

Above him he found a handhold and started to climb. Looking up, he now saw that high above the shaft a great wine-colored Crystal was poised in somber splendor. A beam of violet light shone from the crystal straight down the center of the shaft to the fire below.

As he inched upward, just underneath his feet the fissure was converted into a gaping hole by the impact of a giant claw, which remained protruding into the shaft, blindly snapping for its prey, while the violet beam scorched a smoking hole clean through it.

The Garthim-Master squatted on the front of his throne, a dumbfounded expression in his bulging, baleful eyes. He could not believe what was happening to him. Just when he thought his masterly coup had accounted for the Ritual-Master's pretensions, the situation was deteriorating markedly.

First, he had followed the Chamberlain to the tunnel. What he had expected to find was a Gelfling with enough expiring life in it to yield a plentiful supply of vliya. What he had found instead was a pile of rubble, accompanied by a great wringing of hands on the part of the Chamberlain and a string of lame excuses.

However, he could still anticipate a flaskful from the other wriggling specimen, the one he had entrusted to the Scientist. He had entered the Chamber of Life, intending to imbibe the vliya's rejuvenating powers. Instead, from the doorway he had beheld the spectacle of flocks of wild animals, quite unrestrained, wreaking havoc or escaping through shattered windows, while Aughra sat rocking on her haunches, cackling wildly. Of the Scientist there had been not a sign, nor had he yet reappeared in the ceremonial chambers. Neither had there been a Gelfling or a flask of vliya. It was obvious what stratagem the Scientist had devised. Having released the animals to create a diversion, he was sequestered somewhere enjoying the vliya he had distilled and hoarded for himself. Soon, looking impressively younger, he would swagger in and no doubt lay claim to the throne. It would end in *Haakskeekah!*

The Garthim-Master could not tolerate it. After the ceremony of the Great Conjunction had been completed, he was resolved to take the unprecedented step of setting the Garthim upon a brother Skeksis. He was confident they would not disobey him, although it was a task for which they had not been trained. The Garthim-Master felt quite justified in his decision. It might even increase his popularity among the other Skeksis, but in any event it would make him more respected.

At once the Ritual-Master had assessed matters and started to capitalize on them. Mincing up and down the chamber, he stuck his beak into the ear of any Skeksis that would listen and reminded him that he had been for the immediate sacrifice of the Gelfling. The Garthim-Master caught the eye of the Ritual-Master, who was urgently whispering to the Treasurer as he fingered his knife and looked toward the throne. The Treasurer nodded.

PLAN VIEW

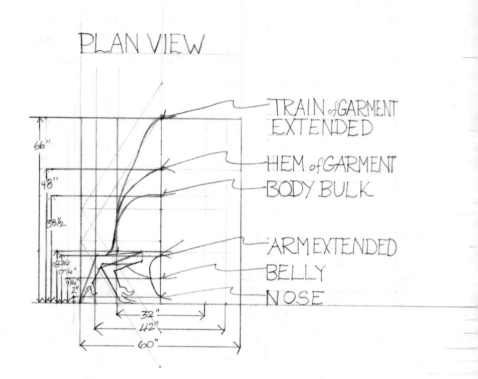

TRAIN of GARMENT
EXTENDED

HEM of GARMENT

BODY BULK

ARM EXTENDED

BELLY

NOSE

66"

48"

58½

18¾
17¼
9¾"
2"

32"

42"

60"

SKEKSIS · GARTHI

Brian Froud

SIDE

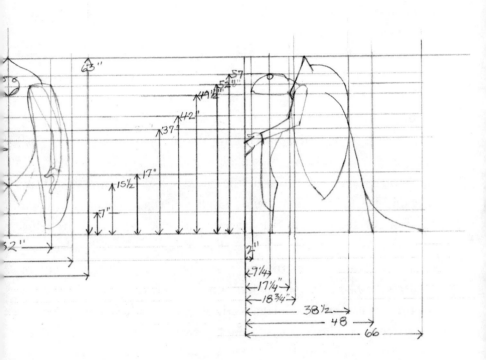

43"
57
52"
49½"
42"
37"
17"
15½
7"
32"
2"
9¼
17¼"
18¾"
38½
48
66

ASTER   scale: ½" = 1'

The Garthim-Master leaned forward and groaned. The old Emperor had never had to contend with this sort of factioning. What could he do with the Great Conjunction imminent?

The Garthim-Master would have been even more astounded if he could have seen outside the castle entrance. The urRu were approaching the end of their trek.

Since the division after the Great Conjunction eons ago, the Skeksis had left the urRu to themselves in their valley. They had to: the object and its mirror image could not be combined except in cancellation of both. In any case, the Skeksis never had needed the urRu: impractical, old, chanting visionaries, obsessed solely with their collective inner life, their values diametrically opposed to those to which the Skeksis ascribed.

Shortly after the division, the Skeksis had discovered that by breaking the Crystal they could entrap malevolent energies that, on the molecular level, were visible as the dark coloring it took on. After some research, the Scientist had explained that the Crystal had a spiral linkage in its molecular structure from which it derived the property of rotating the plane of polarization of a beam of polarized light. When the three suns were conjoined directly overhead, such a polarized power emanated from them that it would untwist the spiral linkage, clear the crystal of color, and produce a focused beam of the most intense concentration. But once the Crystal had been broken, its spiral linkage could not be untwisted. The light of the Great Conjunction would irradiate the Skeksis with energy, but a left-handed energy only, darkly colored, rich in malevolence.

The Skeksis had profited prodigiously from the knowledge and from their control of the Crystal within the fortress they had carved from the mountain that contained it. Along all the ley-lines of energy around the planet, they had continuously fed noxious pulses, fomenting misery and weakness throughout the world. And along the same ley-lines they had sucked in the geodynamic energies. The lightning Jen had seen was focused into the Standing Stones and transmitted to the castle. The Skeksis controlled the nodal points of the planet by terrestrial acupuncture.

Thus it was that the Skeksis had always been able to ignore the urRu. The spy crystals had never monitored them, nor had they been visited by Garthim. Apart from the Standing Stones, nothing at all in that valley ever could have represented a threat to the empirical tyranny of the Skeksis. The valley of the urRu was an enclave of notions, the province of clouds, nothing more.

In the sky, the three suns were no more than their own diameter apart. With infinite weariness, leaning on their sticks, the urRu filed slowly down the slope toward the castle gate.

Inch by inch, Jen climbed the shaft, clinging grimly to any holds the rock offered his fingers and toes. He tried to keep his concentration fixed on the stone walls, watching out for dangerously loose patches. He did his utmost to resist looking upward to see how far he still had to go to reach the Crystal, or downward to see the lake of fire that awaited an error of judgment, a moment of weariness. His limbs ached horribly.

He became aware of an intermittent noise not far above him. Sometimes it sounded like snorting, at other times like a cackle. He risked a look upward. Just over his head, he saw an opening in the wall of the shaft next to him. He took heart. It would afford him a place to rest, at least. The noise was evidently coming from whatever lay behind the opening.

When he was level with it, he gripped the ledge with one hand and swung his other hand over to join it. Hauling himself up, he crawled into the Chamber of Life, through the portal that had remained open since the Scientist's fall.

The chamber was deserted, though it was apparent that, shortly before, it hadn't been. Cages hung open; straw littered the floor; retorts, jars, and cabinets lay smashed. Jen heard the snorting sound again and wheeled around to see what it was. Amid the chaos sat Aughra, scrutinizing the Scientist's books with keen appetite. The pockets of her tunic bulged with pieces of apparatus and veined stones which she had appropriated from the abandoned laboratory.

"I"–Jen began–"I thought you were dead. In the fire at your Observatory."

Aughra cackled. "Better hurry," she replied. "Not much time now, Great Conjunction. Miss that, wait another thousand years, ha!"

"'*When single shines the triple sun,*'" Jen quoted.

"Yes, yes," Aughra said impatiently. "No time. Get to Crystal."

Jen stretched his tired limbs. With a deep breath of determination he moved back toward the portal and the shaft leading up to the Crystal.

Aughra intercepted him. "Not there." She pointed to the doorway. "Easier way, through there. Got shard?"

"Yes."

"Good. Very, very interesting. Your friend said you got it."

"Kira?" Jen asked quickly. "Was she here?"

"Yes."

"Is she still alive?"

"Was, in here."

"Where is she? Where did they take her?"

"Went on own, through there. Looking for Crystal, perhaps. Looking for you."

Jen went sprinting through the doorway.

"Go, Gelfling," Aughra muttered to herself.

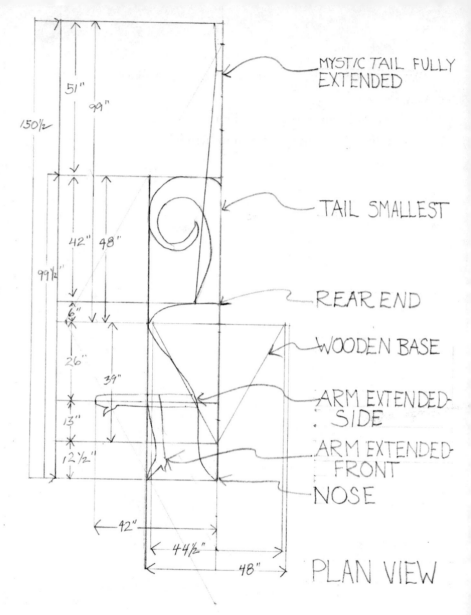

MYSTIC TAIL FULLY EXTENDED

TAIL SMALLEST

REAR END

WOODEN BASE

ARM EXTENDED-SIDE

ARM EXTENDED-FRONT

NOSE

51"

99"

150½

42"   48"

99½"

6"

26"

39"

13"

12½"

← 42" →

← 44½" →

← 48" →

PLAN VIEW

MYSTIC   scale: ½" = 1'

Brian Froud

CHAPTER IX

WHEN SINGLE SHINES
THE TRIPLE SUN

The Garthim-Master retired to his bedchamber. Scepter in hand, he admired himself in the mirror and began to feel calmer.

It was, after all, understandable that the Skeksis had lately been subject to hysterical fears. At the very end of the solar cycle, their energies were predictably flagging. Soon everything would be under control again. The Garthim-Master would go out and lead them in the ceremony of the Great Conjunction. Freshly endowed with superb strength, the Skeksis would then have nothing to fear. Skeksis rule over the planet stabilized once more, the Garthim-Master's own position as Emperor would be reaffirmed. Just to be sure of that, he would eliminate the Scientist, and he would reward the Slave-Master's loyalty by appointing him to the newly created post of Patriarch, which would be a rank senior to that of both Ritual-Master and Chamberlain. The Garthim-Master wondered if he should not cultivate new allies. The Ornamentalist, perhaps, could be weaned away from the Chamberlain's party.

Deeply moved by his rededication of faith, the Garthim-Master continued to gaze at himself in the mirror and clutched the scepter more tightly than ever.

Outside the castle entrance Garthim formed a solid line of defense against all intruders. Their claws bristled out in front of them.

At the foot of the slope, the approaching urRu resembled pilgrims completing the penitential journey of their long lifetime. Their great, tired heads were now held much lower than the hands with which they gripped their walking sticks. So dusty were their garments that nothing could be seen of urUtt's complex weaving and knotting. Led by urZah, they looked neither to the left nor right. Their eyes were fixed on the ground in front of them. Their tails dragged behind. They headed straight for the castle entrance.

Overhead, the three suns were almost touching.

When the urRu were but four weary steps away from the Garthim, urSol sang out a mighty note. The other seven raised their voices with his in a polyphonic chord of the utmost majesty. It was the nine-toned chant, the resonance of the great Crystal. From where did the ninth voice come? It might have been that urSol himself was chanting a chord. Or the ninth voice might have responded from within the castle itself. Only the urRu knew. But whatever the explanation, the effect was immediate. The Garthim, creatures of the Skeksis, abominators of the sound of the unclouded Crystal, lowered their claws and shuffled meekly away from the entrance, allowing the chanting urRu to pass through without hindrance.

In Jen's hand, the shard was glowing with a cold, pale fire. He looked at it in awe of the shard's intrinsic power and of what the shard told him. His time had come. Whatever his doubts and weaknesses hitherto, there was no turning back now. He was irrevocably committed to accomplishing the final stage of his quest. No longer did he feel any fear. All he felt was that, like a spear launched, he had a single objective. He would succeed or he would fail: those were the terms of his existence, and no others.

With the marvelous, dispassionate clarity of the concentrated mind, he was fully conscious of what else he valued. He hungered for the sight and the touch of Kira, or at least the knowledge of what had become of her. Yet, Kira, and his care for her, was as if part of another life, an alternative life, past for sure, possibly a future to come, infinitely more desirable than what he had now to do; but until he had accomplished his mission, he had no more choice than the spear in flight.

Running from the Chamber of Life he had encountered only a few Pod slaves, who had taken no notice of him. He came to the balustraded lower gallery of the Crystal Chamber and from there stared up at the great Crystal suspended in air. Wondering how to reach it, he caught sight of the high balcony beside the Crystal and realized that there must be a way up to it.

He left the gallery, made his way along a corridor, and turned a corner. In front of him stood ten Garthim, five on either side of the foot of a staircase leading upward.

Jen spun around in midstride and sprinted back to the corner of the corridor, his heart thumping, his hand grasping the shard like a dagger. At the corner he threw a glance over his shoulder. What he saw was that the Garthim had not moved. They were still positioned exactly where they had been.

Jen waited to see how many of them would pursue him. Still none of the Garthim moved. They stood at the foot of the staircase like hollow suits of armor. Nor, he realized, were they emitting the ticking

Brian Froud

noise that always preceded their onslaughts.

Very tentatively he took a step back toward them, then another. Not one of the Garthim moved or showed any sign of life.

Knowing that he had to find his way up to the high balcony, Jen steeled himself to go on stepping, on tiptoe, toward the staircase between the Garthim. Coming within a claw's reach of them he held his breath. Then he skipped between the two lines and ran up the stairs. Still none of them gave any indication of registering his presence.

The truth, which Jen could not know, was that Garthim did what the Skeksis ordered them to do and nothing more. Those from whom Jen had narrowly escaped in the Garthim pit had recently returned from the raid on Kira's village and so were still under orders to seek and destroy Gelfling. But these, stationed around the corridors of the castle, had no orders at present. They had been posted in readiness for any emergency that might arise. Until the Garthim-Master or another Skeksis commanded them into action, they were lifeless.

Along corridors and up staircases Jen ran. Glimpses of the Crystal through archways that he passed sustained his sense of direction. Outside a large door he encountered another squad of Garthim and tiptoed past with trepidation. When these did not move either, Jen wondered if his fight in the Garthim pit had in some way served to immobilize the force. Nevertheless, his heart pounded each time he passed another squad.

Ascending every staircase he saw, he finally ran up a short flight of steps to find himself on the high balcony. The vision of the huge Dark Crystal in the air, so close in front of him, was awesome. And there, exactly where the fresco at the Gelfling ruins had pictured it, was the gash in the Crystal, the wound at the core of being. Like the shard in his hand, it seemed to be throbbing with longing to be healed. For one brief moment, Jen wondered if his shard would magnetically lodge itself in the wound were he just to throw it where it belonged.

Gazing downward, he knew he could not risk anything so hazardous. Almost directly beneath him he could see the upper opening of the shaft that he had partly climbed; from inside the shaft it had not been possible to appreciate how far short of the Crystal itself it terminated. If the shard hurtled down there, into the lake of fire, the world would be irreversible.

With his eye, Jen measured the distance between the balcony and the Crystal, and reckoned he would not be able to jump it. What was also difficult to gauge was how he would cling to the polished, sloping facets of the Crystal long enough to restore the shard. As for where his feet would find the purchase to launch him back to the balcony again, that was no concern of the spear in flight.

Spread out below him was the triangular chamber with the elaborate, spiral pattern filling the floor. At present it was deserted, but he supposed that it would not be so for much longer. Above the Crystal, the portal in the roof was open, and in each corner of it stood a sun. The event that Aughra had prefigured with her eye looking through her brass triangulum—pupil, iris, ball concentrating—must soon be due.

Having failed to find her way back to the tunnel where Jen was buried, Kira had hidden herself in a niche behind a tapestry on the wall of a corridor. There she had rocked herself in a misery of despair beyond tears. No Jen, no shard, no village to return to—nothing, nothing remained. Now she almost regretted that she had ever met Jen. Until then, she had lived without hope. There had been no need for hope, nothing to hope for. Her life had been contentment, the daily, seasonal round of Pod existence. This, she had assumed, was how it would always be, and she had made no mental picture for herself of how it might otherwise have been. True, she, like Jen, had sometimes indulged in a fantasy, born of her infant trauma, that other Gelfling might one day appear. She had seen the marriages and the couplings of the Pod People, and understood that, in a different world, she also might have bred children. But the spirit of the Pod People's life took as little heed of the future as it did of the memoried past, and nothing encouraged her to think that her fantasies might paint possibility.

And then Jen had appeared. It was the truth, what she had told him, that her first impulse, in the swamp, had been to run away, silently. She understood why. Jen represented hope; and hope, she instinctively knew, would always be shadowed with pain, just as her despair, now, in the niche behind the tapestry, was shadowed with something like the opposite of pain—a numbed uncaring, an acceptance of the thrall of death, almost a fervent wish for it.

Almost. But when she heard the sound of many feet and voices approaching along the corridor and felt her body tense, she recognized that, beneath her wishing and regrets, the oldest and deepest ordinance of all, the will to survive, was what was causing the tension. If she could escape from the castle, she would. But she had no idea how to escape.

The approaching feet were heavy, but the voices were predominantly light ones, singing a monotonous processional. Very carefully, Kira peered around the edge of the tapestry. Coming toward her were eight Skeksis, followed by a choir of Pod People.

She shrank back behind the tapestry, trembling, while the bodies of Skeksis lumbered past. Such a formal precession, she reflected, was likely a preparation for some important ceremony connected with the Crystal, quite probably related to the Great Conjunction of which she had heard tell. By following the procession, she ought to find her way back to the Crystal. If Jen ever did escape from the tunnel, he would surely try to find his way there as well. And if not—well, wherever the procession led her, it could not be a place of greater despair than where she was now.

She could hear that the Skeksis had passed, and now the Pod choir was just on the other side of the tapestry. She peered out again. From their eyes, she knew they were unredeemed slaves. She could not expect them to do anything for her or to feel anything. But she could hope that they would simply disregard her if she joined them surreptitiously.

Kira stepped out among the chanting slaves, keeping her body slack, her head down, so that she was of similar height. She walked along with them, and they took no notice at all of her. If she kept herself shielded behind her erstwhile friends, she might go undetected by Skeksis or Garthim.

And then, just ahead of her in the procession, she recognized a figure she had known all her life. At once her heart leaped up—it was Ydra, beyond any doubt. With a little sigh, Kira worked her way forward until she was by Ydra's side. She tapped her foster mother on the arm and smiled.

The face that turned to her was Ydra's face, but it wore no expression. The eyes stared milkily at Kira, then were turned forward again.

"Ydra," Kira whispered, "oh, Ydra. It's me, Kira. Don't you know me?"

Ydra's etiolated eyes flickered in her direction, and for a moment the old woman faltered in her singing. Kira realized that by continuing to address her in the tongue of the Pod People she might effect the liberation in Ydra that she had achieved with the wild animals in the Chamber of Life. Deliberately she kept silent. For the present, in this perilous situation, it was better that Ydra, and all the other slaves, should remain as they were. Later, if the opportunity of escape arose,

Kira knew that she could give them the will to seize it.

At the head of the procession, the Skeksis turned through a grand doorway, followed by a number of the slaves. The majority, however, including those around Kira, continued along the corridor, past immobile Garthim, and ascended a staircase. At the top, Kira found herself once again in the balustraded gallery overlooking the Crystal Chamber.

Her eyes were drawn upward to the Crystal and, above it, to the open portal in the roof. The sight of the three suns was oddly encouraging. She knew it portended that something would shortly happen to leave the world altered, utterly. In the winter of hope, the mind craves change.

Around her the Pod choir had formed into rows and was chanting a pompous, triumphant anthem of great monotony. It sounded bizarre sung in their piping voices. Below, on the floor of the chamber, other bands of slaves were marching into position along the walls.

The Skeksis, meanwhile, led by their strutting new Emperor, were parading in a ring beneath the Crystal, croaking harshly in unison with the choir. Following the Emperor, the Ritual-Master and the Chamberlain marched, each trying to wedge his shoulder in front of the other's. Next came the Slave-Master, his unpatched eye glowering around the chamber to warn his helots of the consequences of error. The Ornamentalist followed, glaring at the choir to sing louder. The Treasurer, the Scroll-Keeper, and the Gourmand completed the procession. All of them were at a pitch of excitement. The ceremony would serve a twofold purpose: ritually, it would celebrate and confirm the barbaric power they had over the world; physically, it would recharge their wills so they could continue exercising that power.

The Garthim-Master ascended the dais, the Chamberlain hastened to stand at the right arm of the throne, and the Ritual-Master took up his accustomed position facing the new Emperor. Between them, looks were exchanged—still no sign of the Scientist. Where was he, with that Gelfling? the Garthim-Master puzzled. Vigorous with vliya, would he swoop in at some critical stage and attempt a coup? He could scarcely forego the ceremony altogether. Rejuvenated his body might be, but it still needed the potency that only the tenebrous rays of the Crystal could supply. The Garthim-Master had his Garthim ready, just outside the chamber.

The three suns had started to move toward the middle of the triangular portal in the roof, filling the gleaming Crystal below with dark translucence. Beside it, on the high balcony, Jen could hear that the Crystal was also emitting a sound that was slowly growing louder. It was not the same sound as the shard's response to his flute but a single, deep note; and it seemed to be generating a series of sympathetic tones, very faint, distant. The walls, perhaps, were remembering a decayed chord.

Jen was crouched behind the parapet of the balcony when the Skeksis had entered in procession, beneath him. In response Jen had shrunk back into the shadows. He could still see most of the chamber floor, where the bands of Pod slaves were marching about. When the choir assembled in the lower gallery, across the chamber, Jen watched them without attention while he contemplated what he had to do.

And then, among the Pod slaves, his eye singled out Kira. He stifled an involuntary shout of joy. He dared not attract her attention by calling or gesticulating. Hoping to exploit the channels of dreamfasting, he concentrated his gaze on her and willed a silent message to reach her. "Kira, Kira," he whispered intently.

The Ritual-Master raised his pious hands to commence the formal ceremony. "*Khavekh*," he intoned, "*Khavekh, Khavekh, Orkhasstim.*"

The Ritual-Master's solemn words were still reverberating when suddenly they were drowned by a profane riot of barking. Fizzgig had found Kira at last. He had been wandering the corridors and passages, dodging out of sight of Skeksis, grimacing at Pod slaves, sniffing in corners for a trace of her. On a staircase he had picked up her scent and followed it to the gallery. Now, in an ecstasy of barks, he was romping around her, delighted to see her again and waiting for her to share his joy.

Kira grabbed Fizzgig and tried to stifle his barking. She was too late. The noise had echoed all around the chamber, piercing the thin harmonies of the Pod choir and the intermittent grating of the Ritual-Master's invocation.

The Garthim-Master glared up at the gallery and saw Kira as she strove to silence Fizzgig.

The Garthim-Master bellowed. "*Kelffink!*"

The Garthim outside the chamber door rumbled up the staircase toward Kira's hiding place among the choir.

From the high balcony Jen saw what was happening. Breaking cover, he leaned on the parapet and screamed, "Kira!"

The Garthim-Master glared up again. His eyes popped when he saw the second Gelfling. "Garthim!" he shrieked. "*Teen Kelffinkim!*"

A second detachment of Garthim stampeded through the castle corridors.

Jen's shout had transfixed Kira. She stared up at him with bewildered joy. Even when the Garthim entered the gallery where she stood and started to hunt for the Gelfling among the Pod People, Kira remained where she was. She had to see what happened to Jen. In any event, flight would have been futile.

Her body thrilling, she watched the tiny figure of Jen clamber onto the parapet railing.

He knew it would be only a matter of moments before the Garthim irrupted.

When they did, Jen had no decision to make. His one escape from the Garthim was to jump from the balcony, and the only place to jump was onto the Crystal. Behind him, the Garthim hugely filled the balcony, claws bristling, but they could not follow Jen's example.

Jen landed on the rhombohedral shoulder of the Crystal, all four of his limbs spread, like a frog, grappling for a hold on the shiny geometric planes. His fingers managed to cling, but only at the cost of releasing the shard from his hand.

Like a spinning sliver of light, the shard fell, hit the patterned floor, rebounded in a glittering arc, and came to rest on the very lip of the shaft directly beneath the Crystal.

In the stunned silence on the floor of the chamber, which was only intensified by the continued piping of the Pod choir above as the Garthim ransacked through them, the Ritual-Master was the first of the Skeksis to recognize what the shard was and how appallingly close the prophecy had come to being fulfilled. In an ear-scouring screech, he delivered his awful warning. *"Klakk smaithh Skwee Kreh!"*

From high above them, Jen, sick with failure, gazed down and saw what happened next.

Kira jumped from the gallery and fluttered down on her spread wings. Fizzgig, seeing her leaving again, raced down to the chamber floor by way of the staircase. Meanwhile, all of the Skeksis moved toward the shard.

First and swiftest among them were the Garthim-Master, the Chamberlain, and the Ritual-Master. All three burning to be saluted as the savior of their race, they jostled and impeded each other in grabbing for the shard. As a result, Fizzgig, bouncing into the chamber, was the first to reach it. He sniffed at it anxiously, wondering why neither Jen nor Kira was with it.

And then, with a pull at his heart, Jen saw Kira land and run across the chamber toward Fizzgig and the shard.

The Garthim-Master, as the strongest of the Skeksis, was the one who prevailed. His talons closed around the shard; and as they did so, Fizzgig, now beside himself with anxiety and confusion, bit the Garthim-Master's arm.

The Garthim-Master let out a snarl of pain and flapped his arms angrily. Fizzgig was thrown off-balance, and with one howl he vanished down the shaft, at the foot of which the lake of fire awaited him.

Fizzgig's intervention had left the shard lying unattended. It was Kira, darting between the colossal bulks of the Skeksis, who retrieved it. She wheeled round, her back to the shaft, and, as she had seen Jen do, held the shard out like a dagger.

In the triangular portal in the roof, the three suns overlapped. Beneath Jen's body, the Crystal was humming more loudly.

The Skeksis were watching Kira and the shard with beady, glistening eyes. Their talons itched to grab, but they made no assault. The Ritual-Master, however, was shuffling around to one side of her, and the Slave-Master was moving along the other flank. Kira stood there, turning quickly from side to side, jabbing the shard at them menacingly. The Garthim-Master squatted in front of her, his eyes bulging with baffled fury. Beside him, the Chamberlain had a cunning look.

"They're afraid," Jen said to himself. Then, whoopingly, he called down, "They're afraid of you, Kira! Afraid of the shard!"

Kira's attention was momentarily distracted by Jen's shout. As her eyes flickered up to him, the Ritual-Master's talons savagely raked at her. She saw him just in time, whirled around, and slashed at his arm.

She made only a glancing contact, but the Ritual-Master recoiled as though from a powerful shock. The shard emitted a resonant note. Jen felt the great Crystal vibrate in sympathy.

The Chamberlain tentatively extended his hand toward Kira. He spoke in the wheedling tone that Kira had heard before, at the Gelfling ruins. "*Kelffink*," he cajoled, "gif to me the piece of crystal. Yes, and you go in peace. That is promise I made for you, no? Peace for Skeksis and the little *Kelffinks*. Gif to me, now."

"No," Kira said. She jabbed the shard toward his outstretched hand and threw a rapid look up at the portal. The three suns were almost as one.

Jen saw her glance, the turn of her head toward him. He realized what she intended. And he saw the sunlight flash on the long blade of the sacrificial knife the Ritual-Master had drawn. He cried, "Kira! Give it to them!"

The Chamberlain turned his neck to look up at Jen. Nobody else on the chamber floor moved. The Pod choir piped on.

"Don't hurt her," Jen shouted to the Chamberlain. "You can have the shard. Let her go!"

The Chamberlain looked back to Kira, with a smile.

Kira stared straight into the Chamberlain's eyes while she called up, "No, Jen. Heal the Crystal."

Jen saw her draw her arm back holding the shard. She turned her face up to him. He was crying, "No, Kira, they'll kill you!" as she threw the shard back up to him.

In a high, slow arc, the shard glittered through the air, toward the cavity in the Crystal, and curved into Jen's hand. As he caught it, he looked below and a long moan of despair filled his throat. His gaze was fixed on Kira's face, smiling up to him, as the Ritual-Master stabbed his sacrificial knife through her back.

Below, around Kira's body, he saw faces of the Skeksis staring up at him. He regarded the shard with loathing. To drive it back into the Crystal, to heal the wound, he raised his arm.

Suddenly, he could not see. There was too much light. The beam of the concentric suns hit his face.

Blindly, he plunged the shard down, in deep.

The great Crystal flashed. With the flash came a high-pitched, bell-like boom of thunderous intensity.

Jen's fingers slipped from the reverberating surfaces. Already senseless, he fell down through the dazzled air. His fall was broken by the body of one of the Skeksis. Jen rolled down to the floor of the chamber and lay beside Kira.

None of the Skeksis moved toward him. All eight were crouched with their hands over their ears, their eyes squeezed shut in agony.

Only the Pod slaves were clearly aware of what was happening. The Dark Crystal had cleared to a lucent transparency. Within it, the deeply cracked and fissured interior was revealed, but already it was being reamalgamated to its perfection by the energy of the Great Conjunction, shining in a triple column, dark, rose, and radiance itself. From the Crystal, the light was refracted into beams that slanted sharply downward, each of piercing intensity.

The Pod slaves saw each other's milky eyes clearing, becoming black buttons again. They saw Garthim claws dropping off, armor plates hitting the floor with a clatter, and extinguished purple eyes. Soon, nothing was left of the Garthim but heaps of shell. Awakened dreamers, the Pod People stared with moon-blank faces as the very walls of the castle started to quake. The encrusted filth of centuries was shaken off, disclosing the pure, crystalline beauty of the original fabric, the living stone of the mountain. The harmony of the sunlit Crystal

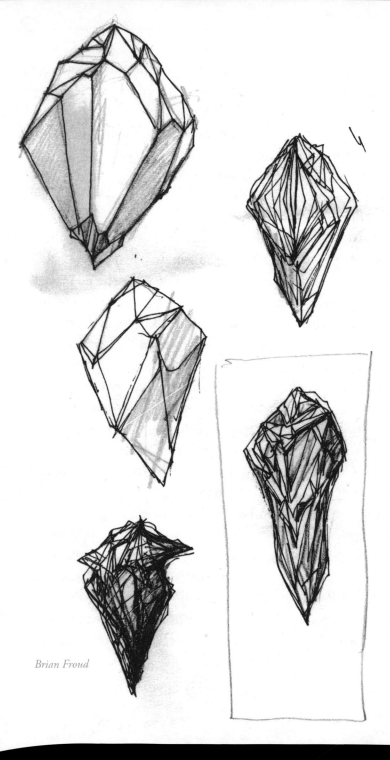

Brian Froud

resonated along ley-lines all around the planet, remitting the evil of the rule of the Skeksis.

In the Chamber of Life, Aughra, too, felt the rumbling. "Ah!" she gasped. "At last!" As she hobbled toward the door, an indignant yapping behind her made her pause. She turned and saw Fizzgig in the open portal of the shaft, his paws clinging around the rod with the crystal prism at its end.

"Pah!" Aughra snapped impatiently, but she picked up a long wooden fork and crossed the laboratory. She thrust the fork into the shaft, hoping to reach Fizzgig. He growled at the fork, seeing it not as an implement of rescue but as a weapon. Only when Aughra attempted to leave him did he consent to bounce along the fork to safety.

Then Aughra made her way to the door. Fizzgig followed. "At last," she was crooning, "at last. Aughra now see it again. For this saved my eye."

On the floor of the chamber, Jen had regained consciousness. He was on his knees, sobbing with grief, as he cradled Kira's lifeless body in his arms. He was oblivious of the events around and above him.

Into the quaking, brilliant chamber strode the urRu. No longer doddering sages but a liberating army, irresistible as truth, they entered giving full voice to their majestic eight-toned chord, over which the ringing of the Crystal sang a ninth at the octave. As the urRu marched in, the Skeksis scuttled away from them in terror. They could not escape from the radiance of pure white light that now streamed through the castle walls where the putrid rubble had fallen away.

Fizzgig raced past them to join Jen and Kira.

Aughra stood at the periphery of the chamber, directly in one of the beams from the Crystal, and gazed fully into the light, her eye not blinking lest she miss a moment. She would live forever, imparting her erratic knowledge of it all.

The urRu had formed an arc on the chamber floor, below the Crystal, each of them positioned in a beam. The light refracted from the Crystal pierced directly through the bodies of the urRu, slanting downward to form pools of intensity on the floor behind them. Toward these pools the eight Skeksis were ineluctably drawn, as though by a vacuum. They writhed and collapsed on the floor, hissing horribly.

Meanwhile, continuing to sustain their mighty chant, the urRu swayed their bodies to a mesmeric rhythm in the beams that transfixed them.

When each paralyzed Skeksis arrived at his destined pool of light, he too was impaled on the beam and drawn up it, toward his urRu counterpart, until they were each fused as a single creature, an urSkek, as in the past and to be, the two made one. Beings that seemed distilled from golden light rather than made of substance, the urSkeks stood tall and erect in an arc below the brilliant Crystal.

Through his sobbing, Jen heard a voice call him. "Gelfling, listen to me." He looked up. The urSkek in whom urIm the Healer and skekUng the Garthim-Master were united was addressing him, while it swayed in the beam from the Crystal, visible energy pouring from its head. In its face were combined the wisdom of the urRu and the knowledge of the Skeksis.

Holding Kira's body in his arms, Jen stood up, and through his tears faced the arc of chanting urSkeks.

The one that had addressed him spoke again. "We are urSkeks. Long ago, in our folly and our ignorance, we almost destroyed this world. We entered the great Crystal, intending to purge ourselves of the imperfections within. Instead we shattered the Crystal—and ourselves—into urRu and Skeksis. But the world we sundered has been made whole by your courage, your sacrifice. You have freed us from this world again, to return to the next world, rejoined in our original form. Now we make you again one. Hold her to you. She is part of you as we all are part of each other. You restored the true power of the Crystal. Make your world in its light."

The urSkek raised its translucent hand, deflecting the beam of light onto Kira, who moved in Jen's arms and opened her eyes, her wound healing. The chant reached a climax.

Clasping each other, Jen and Kira watched as the urSkeks traveled up along the beams of light and, entering the Crystal, apocalyptically transformed, passed through it into another astral dimension.

The chamber was silent. The three suns above the Crystal moved out of their Great Conjunction.

THE END,
at which the endless spinning world
enjoins a new beginning...

THE END

BEHIND A.C.H. SMITH'S
THE DARK CRYSTAL
NOVELIZATION

When Jim Henson sought a writer to transform his epic fantasy film, *The Dark Crystal*, from vibrant images on the screen to enthralling words on the page, he found just the right man for the job: A.C.H. Smith. Known to his friends as Anthony, Smith was and is a prolific novelist, playwright and poet, working in Bristol and London. He studied at Cambridge and contributed to numerous poetry and prose reviews in the 1950s and '60s, becoming active in the vibrant Bristol literary scene. Smith collaborated with Tom Stoppard on various projects, and rubbed elbows with a who's who of writers including Ted Hughes, Sylvia Plath and Samuel Beckett. All the while, Smith followed his keen interest in cricket and wrote about it for the *London Times*. His novels, plays and poetry received critical acclaim, but it is among his five novelizations, especially the two for Jim Henson, where Smith has found his greatest commercial success. He continues to write for theater and recently published a memoir, *Wordsmith*, which provides an entertaining account of his career and philosophy on writing.

As Smith described in an interview last year, it was standard practice in the 1970s and '80s for the release of a feature film to be accompanied by the publication of a related novelization. Along those lines, the publishing division of Jim Henson's company produced numerous Muppet publications including storybooks based on his first two feature films, *The Muppet Movie* (1979) and *The Great Muppet Caper* (1981). Jim was enthusiastic about products and books inspired by his characters, appreciating them as alternate ways for fans to interact with his creative vision. A novelized version of *The Dark Crystal* was an ideal method to further express the imaginative energy that went into the film and to place the complicated mythology that he had developed with designer Brian Froud into the company of established fantasy literature.

In the process of creating *The Dark Crystal* film, Jim hired linguist (and children's fantasy author) Alan Garner to create a unique language for the decadent and villainous Skeksis. When it came time to find an author for the novelization, Jim naturally thought to ask Garner if he would take on that task, too. Garner declined, occupied with his work on his own fiction, but suggested Bristol-based documentary filmmaker Michael Croucher for the job. Croucher was approached, and turning it down, he suggested A.C.H. Smith who had recently done the novelization of the seven-part mini-series *Edward and Mrs. Simpson*. Smith certainly knew Jim's work and was delighted to take on the project.

Smith's experience on *The Dark Crystal* was unlike anything he had done with people in the film industry previously. Reflecting on it thirty years later, Smith explained, "[Jim] was a charming man, but what mattered was that, unlike most people who commission novelizations, he cared about the book, as a legitimate child of the movie, as he cared about the film." It was not typical for a director/producer to take such a strong interest in the novelization of a film, but Jim was deeply concerned about "giving his audience the real thing." Smith described being given "scripts, think papers, and designs" to base his novel on and being brought up to the studio to see the puppets and sets and watch the film in production. Jim read the manuscript and wrote extensive, thoughtful notes explaining areas that he thought should be "tweaked" or handled differently. After submitting those notes (which are now housed in the Harry Ransom Center at the University of Texas and transcribed in this volume) to Jane Leventhal, head of Henson publishing, Jim invited Smith to meet. Over lunch, they discussed the book and Jim made some additional suggestions. Smith noted that Jim was "a very nice bloke, great to work with," and Smith appreciated the "fair amount of trouble that Jim had taken" to provide feedback. Smith enjoyed watching and collaborating with the whole Henson team, remarking that he had, "the pleasure of working with very professional people" in all areas – whether the production crew or the publishing department – and that they all, mirroring Jim's style, worked very "gently and subtly."

Clearly, Jim enjoyed the process, too, and noted that, "There were things that we talked about putting into the film that never got in here, which could go into the book." In his comments on the swamp scene, for example, Jim suggested that Smith describe some of the unused ideas for fanciful flora and fauna and natural effects as a way of fleshing out the story a bit. Smith's first draft was based on early versions of the scripts, so Jim's careful reading helped Smith capture changes in dialogue, names of characters, and edits in story structure as well as misinterpretations of what he might have seen on set. Jim was adamant that descriptions should not depict things we are familiar with, counseling, "I think that we must make the point that this is not our world." Jim even encouraged Smith to invent words for the "vegetarian kinds of things" the Pod People were eating.

The movie, while not critically acclaimed, did well at the box office and found an enthusiastic audience. This was also true for the novelization, and to Smith's delight, it rose quickly on the *New York Times* bestseller list. There was a large international audience for the film, and the book was published in the U.S., the U.K., France, Spain, Italy, and Germany and was a particular favorite in Japan. Jim was pleased with the process and result and asked Smith to write the novelization for his next fantasy feature, *Labyrinth*.

Karen Falk
Archives Director, The Jim Henson Company
Long Island City, New York

Information about A.C.H. Smith can be found on Anthony Smith's website www.achsmith.co.uk *and by listening to Sam Downie's 2012 interview with Smith about the novelizations of both* **The Dark Crystal** *and* **Labyrinth** *at* archive.org/details/HensonCompanyInterviewWithAchSmithNovelistForLabyrinthAndTheDark.

NOTES FROM JIM HENSON ON
THE DARK CRYSTAL

A transcription of Jim Henson's notes and thoughts on A.C.H. Smith's first draft
of *The Dark Crystal* novelization, detailing his vision for the world of Thra.

TO: Jane
FROM: Jim
RE: First Draft of Dark Crystal Novelization

Several of the things I have to say really to the overall
structure of the land or the castle where things are
things like that. Others relate more directly to just
words in the manuscript.

Let me begin with one area that I feel isn't quite
accurate in terms of the castle itself. The crystal is
suspended in the crystal chamber. We call it different
names, and I don't really care what it's called, but
the room itself is triangular in shape, the walls are
triangular and they go up toward the top and there is a
triangual hole in the top. I'm not sure that you can tell
that from the film. There are balconeys along the side of
it at different hieghts--there are two different height
balconeys, but the crystal itself is suspended by energy
forces a few feet from the floor in that center shaft that
runs through that. Now that shaft goes down into the

castle, and the laboratory, or the chamber of life, is off of that shaft, so there is a prism that sticks out into that shaft that sends the rays into the chamber of life and further down the Garthim nest was also adjacent to the shaft and that was how broke out into that. In the throne room, the intent is that the throne room is a different room, and you have to go from the throne room into the corridor and down to the crystal chamber, which happens at one point when the crystal sends out a signal. The funeral is also in a different room.

In this initial power ceremony as described--talks about a throne being empty and that is not quite accurate.

Page 3: This relates to the geography of it all, and I will probably have a couple more note about geography, but in the top para. on p. 3 Jen says that he could see the castle. Our intent was that actually when you're in Mystic Valley, the only way you could see the castle was if you went up to the very top rim of Mystic Valley, then you probably could see the castle. I'm not sure Jen has ever been up to that top rim before. In theory, his life has always been sheltered down in the valley itself. This also relates to when Jen leaves the valley, he has to climb up to the top rim and then he has to climb down, and it is quite a ways down, and he hits bottom in and an area probably of lush green before he starts climbing back up Aughra's mountain. I'm not quite sure that's accurate in this also.

Page 3: There is a note that the crystal is suspended by black chords, but as I mentioned above, it should be energy. I have a feeling that this was something that showed when we shot it, but I don't think so.

Page 4: It talks about to one side of the shaft opened a vass ceremonial chamber, and that is not accurate, because the ceremonial chamber was surrounding the shaft. The shaft is dead center in that triangular floor. Third para. mentions the finest ceremonial robes of the Skekses. Our thinking about the Skekses is that the clothes that they are wearing have been accumulated over the many years, and they put on one layer, and then they put on another layer and that is followed by another layer. They probably seldom take anything off. They don't put on special garments for a special occasion, but in fact, they have tiny little bodies, which have been built up because of the layers of clothes they have put on over the years.

There are several times where I have the feeling that the dialogue should be adjusted in the manuscript (the dialogue in the final film has been changed quite a bit) to reflect the changes which have been made in the film. You should know about the changes in dialogue so that you have the option of adjusting it.

On Page 7, at the bottom of the page where Jen is talking to Ur-zah that dialogue has changed quite a bit.

Page 10: There is a reference to 999 years. We have tryed not to use the term years, thinking this was something relating to our world and our sun going around the earth once every 365 days. In fact, here we have three suns, which is one of the reasons that year doesn't quite work. That could be argued.

Page 11: In the conversation with his Dying Master, Ur-Su, that dialogue also has changed. You might want to look at that.

Page 14: The way the Dying Emperor's body falls apart-- it was my feeling it is described here like a rotting fruit, but what we are trying to do is as though the body hardened and then solidified, almost petrified and then cracked into pieces of like rock. So this is a slightly different view of it.

We talk about feeding things to the Garthim--Page 16. I don't think the Garthim really eat. That humanizes them more than we need to.

Page 17: 2nd para. There is a reference to the Pod People being lobotomized. I think that's not a good description. We have drained a lot of life forces from them, leaving them in that state, but that description just doesn't seem correct to me.

Page 18: This is reference to my early reference to the castle, because the crystal is not in the same room where the funeral takes place.

Page 26: I am slightly uncomfortable with the description of the Priest Chamberlain and the General trying to sit in the throne. This was the way we first conceived it in the script, but we ended up doing it a great less farcical. Here it seems a little broad comedy to me, and I don't think these guys would bite each other. This whole description of the Hakskeekah brings to mind something that I don't know if we talked about very much, but it was always our feeling that there were factions withing the Skekses, and we tryed to work this out at least in performance. I don't believe it exists in the script at any point. But we felt that the Ritual Master, the Chamberlain and the Garthim Master should each have their own supporters. So there was three basic factions among those nine Skekses. The Ritual Master had the Treasurer and the Historian as his supporters; the Chamberlain had the Designer and Gourmet; the Garthim Master had the Scientist and Slave Master.

The CHamberlain, as you can see, has a rather weak team, with only the Designer and Gourmet. On his team, he was part of the Dying Emperor, so there were four of them.

There was the Dying Emperor, backed up by the Chamberlain, Designer and Gourmet--the four of them had enough power to outnumber the other two teams of only three each. You can also see how the Garthim Master's teams, being the Scientist and Slave Master, was really quite strong, which helps set him up to be the next in power. This whole power scheme ties into the Hakskeekah itself, because you can then see how the Chamberlain's people will cheer him and boo the Gartim Master; the Garthim Master's team will do just the opposite; the Ritual Master's team will stay basically neutral, cheering any good blow and just sort of yelling for blood.

This is a small note, but on Page 27 there is a reference to pulling the rope from a pulley high on the wall. In effect that rope is set high on a groove in the floor, and one of the slaves pulls up a handle, while one of the other slaves gets on that rope and when they pull that it does all those other things. I'm not sure how much it matters about making all of this stuff accurate to the film. I have mixed feelings myself, because when I some of these areas that are different, I feel that should be changed but I say that after having lived with this film for so many weeks. I may just be reflecting my own feeling about it.

Towards the bottom of Page 27, again there's a difference in the way we did it in the film, because the swords themselves came out on a rack that was part of the rock itself, as opposed to the slave master bringing them forward.

On Page 28 when the General swings in the fifth paragraph, he hits the rock a minute chip of granite flies off, it comes off with a spark which I think is quite nice because I think when these swords strike the rock they should knock off a little spark.

Page 29--Bottom. There is a reference to the High Priest raising his chalice to the Dark Crystal. Again--the crystal is not in that room.

And indeed on page 30, when they are seeing the Gelfling in there. What we had before was a warning sound eminating from the crystal which rings through the whole castle, and they hear that sound and go into the crystal chamber to see what has happened. It is almost like when the bat birds spot a Gelfling that signal is sent to the crystal and a warning tone, almost like an amplification of the crystal zone vibration, tells the Skekses that something is there.

Page 30: When the General calls the Garthim, it says in the deeps of the castle the Garthim came to life, the feeling is that we felt the Garthim would also be stationed all around the castle there, and indeed outside of the crystal chamber there are at least three or six of them stationed immediately outside that, so they are all around in the castle itself. Their normal position is sort of like statues--they look like they are standing suits of armor until they are called to life. Also when the Garthim leave the castle next to the bottom paragraph, it says towards the lowest exit, that exit down there, the vomitory (vomitory is a wonderful word) called the teeth of screech, that area would only go into the cravice that is around that surround the castle, it is almost like a moat. That really wouldn't get you out. Where they would go is down that exit tube, which you have seen in the film itself, and there is virtually only a couple of those tubes going out in different directions out of the castle. They are almost like organic tubes that go down across that moatlike cravice. The tube itself is only wide enough for one Garthim to go through at a time, which makes it easy to defend.

Page 33: Auhgra --reference to her voice--the line says "but it was not a cruel voice", it was out intent to keep the feeling of Auhgra quite ambiguous so that we don't really know whether or not she is good or bad. In effect, it can be a cruel voice at this point, because Auhgra should come one as quite angry and we should not know that she is possibly good at this point.

Page 34: There is a reference to her stained brown tunic, and in effect her garment is sort of a deep wine red if we want to be accurate.

Page 36: 2nd para describing entering into the observatory, I believe Auhgra has already (in the way we did it in the film) through the tunnel and closed the door. Jen walks into the dark tunnel and wanders for a while before the door opens in the front of him. I think not having Auhgra a part of that opening is more dramatic. Next paragraph, in describing the interior of the observatory, it says the sky was painted on the roof of the dome itself, and it was always our feeling that the dome was sort of a translucent sort of thing that provided the light source in the interior.During the day, the daylight would sort of filter through the translucent dome and at night the dome would acutally glow providing light source inside.

Page 38: Half way down, Auhgra says that that was why the Skeses built the observatory for her, I think this has already been talked about a bit but somehow I can't believe the Skeses actually built that for Auhgra. This is probably just a difference in philiosophy. I'm willing to argue this at some point with somebody. Bottom: There is a description of the Alchemist iron triangulum, and in effect we use one that was brass.

Page 39: 3rd para, which is a long rambling speech of Auhgra's beginning with "wait Gelfling" I have the feeling that that dialogue works a great deal better if she does it while she is wandering around, presumably looking for the shards. I think it reads better if it is in that context.

Page 42: There is a description of the shard and it says dagger shaped, clear in color, flawless. We had the feeling, and we built the shards with flaws in them, so it does have cracks going internally within the crystal. The cracks in the crystal and shard heal in the final conjunction.

Page 43: There is (3rd of the way down) a Skekses hitting a big crystal Hakskeekah, they call it. I think that the Hakskeekah itself is merely used in the dual, in other words, when they broke the original crystal that was a different move entirely, and unrelated to Hakskeekah.

Those are my only notes on these pages so far. Generally, I enjoyed reading it and I think it certainly reflects the film very nicely.

. . .

Page 47: As the Urru go to leave the valley, they do the nine-tone chant. Now at this point or on Page 61, it should say that they are leaving because they know the time has come to leave. We should not say exactly what it is time for, but the Urru should have been packing up, closing up their caves. There should be a finality to this departure.

Further down p. 47, the swamp is an area which could use some more description. The swamp life itself, I mean if we are talking about the idea of flushing out the book a little bit more, this is an area that certainly could use more things. There were things that we talked about putting into the film that never got in here, which could go into the book. We talked about the idea of things like a radiation shower where it is almost like a sunspot situation, where there is a certain kind of radiation coming from one of the suns and when that happens there is a kind of electrical crackling in the air which causes certain animals to go inside in their caves and hide, and other animals come out and sort of bask in it. We talked about the idea of certain liquid metals like mercury that sort of wander around in puddles moving across the land. There are other kinds of creatures that were sort of half animal and half plant. There was a stump-like thing that a three-foot tongue flicked out and ate a butterfly. There could be descriptions of the fungus-like things that grow on rotten tree trunks, that would move and sway in the air. There's lot of that kind of thing, which I think would be interesting to describe.

Page 49: When Jen sees the image of the shard, the image that he is seeing, he sees the crystal being struck a great blow, and at the time it is struck, it is sort of like you see a shattered glass go through the whole shard and then it slowly fades. I think him seeing the image in the shard is sort of like looking at a crystal ball and the image you see may half be in your mind and half there. You don't really know whether you see it or not. I think it doesn't happen a second time, and later on I don't believe he can show it to Kira.

Also on Page 49, when he hears the sound, it shouldn't necessarily be a growling, it's just a strange noise in the swamp, it's a noise unlike the rest of the swamp noises and he has the feeling that he has been watched. It's a very uneasy feeling of another creature nearby. It's an inference of the mindspeech that will be happening later. It's the first indication of this kind of thing. A sense of a creature like himself, but he doesn't know that yet.

Page 50: When Fizgig comes out, he is going to come out very suddenly with a very loud roar, it should almost sound like a lion's roar, it's a huge enormous roar which causes Jen to fall backwards. Fizgig's mouth opens and it is filled with several rows of teeth. It is terribly fearsome. We find out later that that is all Fizgig is. He is all mouth and roar, no substance to the threat. It is sort of like a butterfly or moth that have a very fearsome pattern on their wings, but in reality there is no threat there.

Bottom Page 52: What we've done in the film when Jen is sitting in the muck, what Kira does is she calls, she makes the sound and call the Nebri. So when she calls, there is a low rumbling noise from deep under the muck. Jen looks around worried, and when there is a movement down in the mud and the mire, and he feels something and looks around in a panic, it should be a slightly humorous description. The Nebri, a huge grublike thing slowly comes up underneath Jen and Jen finds himself sitting on top of him, eased up out of the mud and sort of falls off of the Nebri onto the dry ground. I think that's a more dramatic thing than what we've done here. We are calling the mindspeech dreamfasting, but I suspect what we will have to do is send the final script that we're using in the film so we can coordinate a lot of this stuff together.

Page 54: The positions of the people in the banquet hall, it's kind of a long table at the center of the table sits the General. The Rites-Master is on his right, the Elixirist is on his left. Just an order for accuracy, at least. A crab renegade from a previous dish came out of hiding and made a run for it, I don't think that should be a crab, it's too ordinary in name. It could be a crab-like hairy insect or make up a name for it.

Page 56: Second line from the top, it's the Rites-Master's line, I'm uncomfortable with all of the Skekses dialogue not being translated. I think more of it should be translated. It's conceivable that we should have only the English, or else the Skekses language immediately followed by what it means. I think that where we can get away with it in the film, I don't think it works in the book this way. We state that Aughra was not on anyone's side in this crisis. I don't think that's true. In reality she is on the Gelflings side, but we don't particularly want the audience to know that.

Page 60: The scene that takes place on the river, that's going to take place on the twilight and the whole scene will have sort of a pink/orange glow to it. I don't believe there's a moon there. It's a very colorful twilight sunset effect. So the two references to moon and moonlight I think are incorrect.

Page 61: The bat bird should be described slowly pulling himself out of the muck at the edge of the river, and reflecting the image of Jen and Kira as they are arriving at the Pod village. I think it is important that we know that this is the time that the Pod village is visible from the river and that the bat bird can see that that's where they're going. It is important that he sees that because that justifies the Garthim raid on the village. In describing the Urru on their journey, it states that they continue the great nine-tone chant, that doesn't quite seem right to me. I wouldn't think that they would do that.

Page 62: When the 2 Gelflings arrive at Kira's village, what happens as they are getting very close to it, all of a sudden a couple of Pod people should pop up out of the undergrowth immediately around them, because the village would have guards posted all around the outer perimeter of the camp, and they would stay in hiding until they see that it is Kira, then they would pop out and be delighted to see her. The effect is somewhat like the descriptions of Robin Hood's camps where there are outer guards and they see people coming.

Page 63: In describing the food, we say gourds, mush, seeds, nuts, fruit, loaves, cakes, milk, yogurt, all of these things sound very much like food of our world and I think there should be other things, probably strange-sounding foods. There are several times where I feel the descriptions sounds too much like things of our world, and I think we must make the point that this is not our world. All these foods should of course be vegetarian kinds of things.

Page 64: Descriptions of the peasants says that they are basically curious. There are a few lines that say they are gifted carpenters and painters. I think that this is not the way I see them. I think they are very simple peasants. Very homespun, they're not craftsmen. I think the furniture that they make has a beautiful simplicity, but it's got to be a very natural simplicity, not something out of an artistic sense but instead a very primal absolute, functional simplicity. The structure of the evening, what we tried for and what I think is a good idea at least, is that the idea is that it is a long evening. It starts with eating and then some music being played, but the whole evening gets slowly noisier and more enthusiastic and the music gets noisier and wilder. I think the shape of this little scene should be that same sort of thing. I don't think Jen would start dancing until quite late in it. I also like what we did in the film where instead of dancing with Kira, someone comes along and I think Idra, Kira's mother, is a good idea here, she come along and pulls him into the dance. I think there's a certain awkwardness and fun in that whole thing. Having the dancing and the whole evening getting noisier and wilder justifies the people being unaware of the Garthim, and I think that happens right in the middle of the very loudest part of the evening.

Page 66: We talked about stuffing them into a sack, Garthim stuffing peasants into a sack. I think instead they are using wicker cages, which are on the backs of some of the Garthim. When Jen and Kira get outside of the building where the dining hall is, the scene outside is also quite wild, with the Garthim smashing the other buildings, smoke pouring out of them. I think I miss not having that whole scene going on with several Garthim around, and then it's one of those guys that spots them. What we are going for here, is that the Garthim really came to get the Gelflings, and so they are looking around, pawing through everyting looking for Gelflings. Once they realize that there are no Gelflings, they start collecting Pod People as slaves so that the raid won't be a total loss.

Page 68: I don't particularly like the Chamberlain trying to talk to them. I think the Chamberlain nearly stopping the Garthim is more effective. It's more mysterious. I think we really don't want to know if the Skekses is good or bad. I think we even want the audience to think that it is conceivable that the Skekses is really a good guy.

Page 69: If it matters it's his right arm that is wounded in the film instead of his left.

Page 70: We talk about the Skekses being the evil, pure eminent, I think that that agains point out too much that the Skekses is totally evil. We really want to keep that ambiguous. At one point in the script we had an indication from Jen in looking at the Chamberlain and saying that there is something vaguely familiar about him harkening to the fact that the Urru and the Skekses, there is a similarity to them. I think that's slightly more interesting and tantalizing than making him this total evil referred to as so monstrously huge and alien

Page 71: In the middle of the page, Kira says the Pod People were never definite about that. I think that to the contrary, Kira knows that all Gelfling have been destroyed by Garthim and Skekses and the Garthim regularly destroy these villages in their slave raids, so she should be very aware of that.

Page 72: Kira is referring to, and it referred to it also earlier, refers to that's what I told you might interest you here. I think Kira came to these ruins because it is secluded and very private place hidden in amongst the forest. The fact that it is a slightly frightening place to her, I think she would not bring Jen here because it might interest him. Also I believe Kira knows that these were the Gelflings that lived there. BUt the whole place is probably treated as a superstitious place haunted by spirits of Gelflings by the Pod People. They would be superstitious people, so Kira would have picked up this sensed superstition and faint dread, so I think that's why she's afraid of the place. I do believe that she knew that it was Gelfling that lived there. Jen, when he wakes up, I think senses the Gelfling. I think one of the things the Urru would have taught Jen is a sense or an ability to sense things not of this world.

Page 79: The Chamberlain says, and you have crystal piece, yes. I think we don't want the Chamberlain to realize that Jen has the shard. That introduces something that I think would become a great deal stronger in the story. I think the Chamberlain would definitely want to get the shard from Jen. So we have purposely not let the Chamberlain ever see the shard. Even when he is stabbed with it. It happens very quickly and he does not even at that point realize that these Gelflings have the shard. That would be too big a deal for him. I think he would react very strongly if he knew that there was a shard involved.

Page 80: We wanted to get the Chamberlain wooing Jen and talking him into giving up and coming with him. It's almost hypnotic. He is gently getting Jen into the mood of going along with it and Kira very strongly jumps in front of Jen to break that sort of hypnotic mood the Chamberlain has created. In the dialogue in the film we have the Chamberlain repeating several times, Please, yes, Please, yes. Then Jen breaks out of it and says no. Even at this point, we still want to keep the Chamberlain ambiguous. The scene as described here, he is too obviously evil.

Page 81: It refers to a jeweler's eyeglass, again, this is too much of this world. Midway down, I think we should be closer to the film in describing the chair that the Scientist puts the Pod People into. It's a large, strangely shaped chair, probably carved out of a large piece of rock or it could be metal, I'm not sure which. There are three of those chairs mounted in front of the opening to the crystal shaft. The peasant is slammed in to that chair and clamped in. We are not using the metal rod situation in terms of getting the droplets of the elixir. Instead, there still is the force field that goes up into a crystal a few inches away from the hand. Sparks jump across this force field into the crystal. It is condensed as it goes through a tube, leading to a flask and it drips out of that into the flask.

Page 82: Bottom talking about some of the animals--a lot of those animals should be healthy. In other words, some of them are waiting to be used for experimental purposes, so that not all of the animals are half dead.

Page 83: Top It says the General very much doubted if he could win a trial of strength. I think the General is very obviously a great deal stronger than the High

Priest. I don't believe this argument here. Bottom: Talking about Augrah's eye was meatily following him, I think we should say that they eye is sitting on a table. It had been taken from her to make her more helpless and it was out of her reach.

Page 85: When the Landstriders come out, they don't come out with incredible speed. They come out sort of quietly. They had been grazing in the woods, walking gently through the woods. There are three adults and a baby Landstrider. They only take two of them, as they each ride one. You have them riding on three, and I think we should stay with two. Kira also says they'll be so happy when I ask them to go to the castle. That seems a little unreal for them to be happy about it because it is a battle which they lose. It's not the kind of battle they would be looking forward to. I don't think they are quite that intelligent either.

Page 85 (middle: she uses string to go around the neck of the landstrider. That doesn't seem necessary to me.

Page 86: A description of the river at the bottom of the ravine around the castle--I don't think there's a river down there. The castle is in such a barren hunk of land. There might be a little bit of water but just a trickle down in there. The bottom of the ravine is as described later--garbage and muck and junk--centuries of junk, garbage and dead bodies. It should be a foul place.

Page 87: Talks about cages on the ground near the bridge. I think in the film this is the raiding party coming back to the castle, and they see them just as they are about to go in through that bridge. There is only one cage. I don't believe the part about emptied sacks and things like that. In this cage there is about 20 pod people instead of a hundred.

Page 88: I didn't particularly like the Pod People falling over the edge with dreadful wails. We could argue that. It seems kind of sad.

Page 89: In particular, I feel that Kiras foster mother Edra should not be killed at this point. As a matter of fact, we had this in the script for a long time; it was a nice element, but we eliminated it from the film mostly because of complications. But what I think would work well in the book is Kira sees Edra, her foster mother, in the cage and is not able to help her, and consequently, she is turned into a slave. When she sees Edra as a slave, she tries to speak to her.

Page 91: In talking about the mouth of this gargoyle face, it would be too small for a Garthim to go and come from. Also, when Kira says, "You're not going to leave me here because I'm not going to be left anywhere until you restore the shard," a line like that sounds too expository. We've avoided lines like that in the film. I don't think we can get away with it in the book either.

Page 92: We had always planned to have some living creatures down in those tunnels, which I think would be quite interesting. They could be certain types of creatures that live there, probably have great big large eyes. I don't these tunnels are places where the Garthim go either. When Jen comes to the three tunnels, at one point, and I think it might work in the book also, he was going to take the shard and balance it in his hand and slowly it would turn and point in the direction he should go. That might be of use.

Page 93: When the Chamberlain shows up, I think to play up the shock of seeing a shadow in front of them and the Chamberlain coming toward them talking. We don't know, again, whether he is good or evil. He grabs Jen and Kira.

I don't think the Chanter would call out with a great deal of pain. The Urru are much more quiet than that and I think they Chanter would merely notice that his hand was bleeding and walk quietly on.

Page 94: In talking about the purposes and reasons for killing the Gelflings, I think the prophecy should figure into this whole question--that the Skekses have tried to eliminate all the Gelflings because of a prophecy. This prophecy should make the Skekses generally frightened of all Gelflings. Only now when the Elixir could help is there a reason not to kill Gelflings.

Page 95: In reference to the next Conjunction, the next Conjunction should actually strengthen them enormously. The Skekses should be looking forward to this next Conjunction as a way of really gaining a great deal of power and strength. We need to set this up so that we have an alternative to a happy ending. We should be able to see that if Jen is unable to get the shard into the Crystal, the power of the next Conjunction would strengthen the Skekses to the extent that they might be in power for hundreds of years. Next to the bottom paragraph of Page 95, when the High Priest interupted in a screech, again I think we should explain more about what he is saying.

Page 96: The Chamberlain in the second paragraph is protesting. What he is saying is that Kira is the prisoner and he should be the one to decide what happens to her.

Page 100: When Aughra is talking to Kira, she actually can see with her eye, even though the eye is on the table, a distance away from her. Further down, there is a reference to the Pod Slaves. I don't think the slaves should be in the room at this point. We eliminated it from the film because of the fact that it is a little too complicated when the slaves were there. I think it is simplier when there are only wild animals that help Kira. The very bottom of 100 talks about glass fronts of the cabinets were shattering. I think that's not like that room to have glass fronts.

Page 101: It gets a little bloody for me when it talks about the animals ripping the flesh from his feet and hungry for his end trails, his head already ablaze as he tittered, to me these phrases a little bit too strong. I'd prefer him to be tripped, attacked losing his balance, falling into the handle of the control thing, then falling into the pit. Bottom: the animals were really the ones who release Kira, and not Aughra. Things like that and the Pod Drummer confuse things a little bit too much.

Page 102: The conversation with Aughra and Kira, I think there is too much talk here. It feels like these guys shouldn't do too much talking at this point. Too much exposition, saying that the shard has to be restored to the big Crystal in time for the Great Conjunction. That kind of stuff is too clear. It is also too rational for Kira. I think she is in semi-shock and her mind in numbed by this whole experience. She should be in a daze.

Page 103: As she leaves the Chamber of Life, she is going upward to the Crystal, and not downwards. The next area, I prefer the way we have it in the film, with Jen getting to the Crystal Chamber before Kira and I think it is also effective in the film, with Kira, while she is wandering around in the corridors, to have the Skekses go past her on their way to the Crystal Chamber. This also tells her where the Crystal is. I think what probably happens is that she comes strolling along, sort of picking her way through those corridors, working her way to the Crystal Chamber. There is something dramatic about that group going by her to the Crystal Chamber.

Page 106: As Jen gets out of the Garthim pit into the shaft, we should describe a little bit more about that shaft. For instance, far below there is a fire, it should be like it is halfway through the earth, that the fire is. As he looks up, he sees the Crystal, but it is far above him. The shaft itself is also a great deal larger than described here. It is approximately ten feet across and here it says there are no footholes, but in fact, there are footholes and handholes along it, so he is able to climb up. There are narrow little ledges and at one point (not in film), his foot slipped and he dangled as he got his grip again. Also at the time he climbs out of the Garthim pit into the shaft, it's described as taking quite a long time, and I think he's got to get out of that Garthim pit very quickly, because otherwise, just while his head is stuck through the hole, I think they would have ripped him in half from behind. So I think he has to scramble through that hole rather quickly, and then finds himself dangling in the shaft.

Page 107: Next to the bottom paragraph, a reference to the Garthim never been programed, I think for the Garthim to be programed, is a little to contemporary a term. Very bottom, not one Garthim had stampeded into the chamber, I think what we felt is that there are hundreds of Garthim in the castle, so that Jen is down there in the Garthim pit, there may be 20 or thirty of them down in there, but that doesn't prevent the fact that the Garthim would still be all around the castle. What we had, which I believe I described earlier, is that we assume there are Garthim stationed every thirty or forty feet throughout the entire Castle. As Jen and Kira go through those corridors, they would tiptoe past the absolutely immobile Garthim who hadn't been called into action. Another nice scary moment is when Jen first sees the Garthim not in motion. At first he is very scared, but then realizes they are lifeless. These Garthim are immediately outside the Crystal Chamber until the Garthim Master calls them, then they burst into life. I think that's another moment of terror for Jen, which comes later on.

Page 108-109: There's a lot of explanatory material here that's very nice. I question whether that is the correct place to put all of that stuff. It seems to stop the flow, and I would think this same material could go a great deal earlier.

Page 110: When Jen finds his way into the Chamber of Life, and we say the joyous havoc was still in full cry, I think it's a great deal more dramatic if the place is absolutely deserted, and he hears a faint little noice, and hears a noise which turns out to be Aughra cackling to herself looking around. She's looking at the Scientist books, she has always been poking through things looking for things she would find useful and sticking them in her pockets. Somehow, I don't quite believe Jen's attitude of I can't go on anymore. It doesn't quite ring true. Although I like his renewed vigor as he leaves, because he hears of Kira. But this mission is much too strong for him to say he can't go on any longer.

Page 112: The General is getting dressed in his imperial robes. I mentioned before that they don't dress into additional robes.

Page 114: We have Kira in the room already when Jen comes in. I think it is more dramatic if it happens as we described it with Jen coming into the empty chamber, the dramatic vision of seeing the large Crystal for

the first time. It should be a big deal as he sees the
Crystal and sees there is a place there where the shard
is missing. Just as he is putting all of this stuff
together, as he is realizing what he has to do, and
trying to figure out how to do it, he then hears the
Skekses entering and shrinks back hiding, then as the
Skekses come out, Kira shows up. He sees her across the
room, but he can't call out to her. I think all of that
is more dramatic. Sending silent messages to Kira,
trying to communicate, and then having Fizgig show
up seeing Kira and barking at her. All of that seems
the most dramatic, and this is the way we did it in
the film. Fizgig would be absolutely delighted to see
Kira, and would make a lot of noise. I also like Kira
leaping down, using her wings to pick up the shard.
It makes a second use of those wings which I think is
quite dramatic.

Page 119: This moment, at the bottom of the page, as the
shard is arching through the air. I think this could be
described more dramatically. This is a high dramatic
point in the film. It is a moment, which should be frozen
in time. Just as this shard is going through the air,
Kira is killed. There's something almost mystical about
that, the shard is neither with Jen or Kira, but while
it is in that space in the middle, that is the time that
Kira is killed. Almost as though had the shard been
with either one of them, this probably might not have
been able to happen. I think Jen catching the shard at
the same time he realizes what has happened to her is
really quite nice. Then raising the shard out in this
whole combination of anger and despair and plunging it
into the Crystal. Also, we wanted to have the effect of
a thunder clap as the shard goes into the Crystal, and
the power of that almost blasts Jen off of the Crystal
and lands him in a heap down below.

Page 120: Talks about the Garthim falling to pieces and

nothing left of them but heaps of metal. I think the Garthim are made more of shell. I don't believe it's metal.

Page 121: Top of page, Aughra has to use some sort of tool or implement to reach over to Fizgig. We like the idea, I'm not sure it shows in the film, she has this wooden fork that she picks up and reaches it over there to get him down and he growls at her. It seems nice that she is trying to rescue an animal and the animal is snarling and growling, not realizing that you are helping him. As Jen is cradling Kira's body, I think it should be described as a lifeless body. We need to make the point that Kira was indeed killed.

Page 122: This whole ending, I think the dialogue that we're using in the film is quite nice, and you should get copies of that. In effect, Jen picks Kira up and walks around to stand in front of the Urskeks who are in a circle and sort of chanting together. That's when the Urskeks speaks to him, calls on him to bring Kira back to life, and as he holds Kira to him, the chanting of the Urskeks behind combine to bring life back to Kira. I think we can make that point more dramatically, then this glory and sort of light show as the Urskeks then disappear up into the sky. It can be described more dramatically.

Transcribed from the A.C.H. Smith Papers (Series I, Subseries A, Box 4, Folder 3-4) in the Manuscript Collection at the Harry Ransom Center, The University of Texas at Austin.

GRAPHIC NOVELS FROM
ARCHAIA AND THE JIM HENSON COMPANY

The Dark Crystal: Creation Myths
Brian Froud, Brian Holguin, Joshua Dysart,
Matthew Dow Smith, Alex Sheikman, Lizzy John

The Power of the Dark Crystal
Simon Spurrier, Phillip Kennedy Johnson,
Kelly and Nichole Matthews

The Dark Crystal Tales
Cory Godbey

Fraggle Rock: Omnibus
Jeffrey Brown, Katie Cook, Cory Godbey,
Jeff Stokely, and More

Labyrinth: Coronation
Simon Spurrier, Daniel Bayliss, Dan Jackson

Labyrinth Tales
Cory Godbey

Jim Henson's The Storyteller
Witches, Dragons, Giants, Fairies
Jeff Stokely, Daniel Bayliss, Conor Nolan,
Tyler Jenkins, and More

The Musical Monsters of Turkey Hollow
The Lost Television Special by Jim Henson & Jerry Juhl
adapted by Roger Langridge

Jim Henson's Tale of Sand
The Lost Screenplay by Jim Henson & Jerry Juhl
as realized by Ramón K. Pérez